The Grumpy Driver's HANDBOOK

This book is dedicated to Geoffrey 'Beaver' Hopkinson – a motor trade legend in his own considerable lunchtime.

Produced by Salamander Books, 2009

First published in the United Kingdom in 2009 by
Portico Books
10 Southcombe Street
London
W14 0RA

An imprint of Anova Books Company Ltd

ISBN 9781906032791

A CIP catalogue record for this book is available from the British Library.

10 9 8 7 6 5 4 3

Printed and bound by WS Bookwell, Finland

This book can be ordered direct from the publisher.
Contact the marketing department, but try your bookshop first.

www.anovabooks.com

The Grumpy Driver's HANDBOOK

Ivor Grump

PORTICO

CONTENTS

INTRODUCTION

With a surname like mine you tend to get tarred with a certain kind of brush. So I need to make it quite clear from the very start that this is not a book wallowing in misery. My brother Arthur, the author of *One Grump or Two*, produced a truly depressing tome full of pedantry on an epic scale. Grump is an inadequate description to describe him; "career miserable bastard" is much more appropriate. No, throughout this book you will find moments of great joy and delight, especially when some coffin dodger has stuffed their Honda Accord into the wrong end of the car wash and jammed the rollers.

I like to think my exploration of Britain's motoring foibles is, "Lighting the path to a greater understanding of the motoring psyche and establishing innovative new rules for the road." Or, at least, that's the quote I'm going to suggest some motoring name endorses on the cover. Obviously, with the kind of money my publisher has available, we can't afford any of the *Top Gear* boys. Even *Fifth Gear* might be out of our reach and we will have to go for something like "The Fat One" from *Deals on Wheels*.

This book is an investigation of the many quirks and idiosyncrasies of the great British driver. As Mr Toad would say, "Motoring's the life, Ratty, poop poop!" In fact, there are a lot of erstwhile Mr Toads included within these pages; lane hoggers, lane cheaters, cat's-eye cleaners, flashers, bumper huggers, drive encroachers, space stealers, and they are all dealt with in withering fashion.

You see, the trick when dealing with a subject that gets us hot under the collar is to imagine what would happen to the troublemakers if summary justice prevailed. Throughout this book you will see what could happen in the Republic of Grump. Drivers would live in fear of losing their cars to *the crusher* in the same way that parents feared the child catcher in *Chitty Chitty Bang Bang*. But only if you are a lazy, inconsiderate, selfish car snob. If you are a law-abiding motorist with an average car driven in a courteous and friendly manner you have nothing to fear under the new regime. It's the others we're out to get.

The Grumpy Driver's Handbook is a manifesto for changing the rules of the road. If you recognise any of the people described in the following chapters, show them a copy of this book. You will be doing them an enormous favour, even if it does mean missing out on the odd Christmas card or two.

FEATURES INCLUDE...

Car Radios

You'd think it would be nigh on impossible to hate a car radio. But you'd be wrong, of course. Car radios are sent to try us. For a start they make the dreadful assumption that the person in control is sitting in the passenger seat, and so they put the volume control on the left-hand side and not the right. The driver's in charge of the vehicle and by default should be in charge of volume!

This gives rise to those dangerous leaning moments, when you'd really like to listen to a certain news item, or the weather, and lean across to turn it up. If you keep your eyes steadfastly on the road ahead then you end up jabbing one of the pre-set buttons and turning to Classic FM (it came pre-installed and you don't know how to change it). Now you're annoyed. Oh yes, you are. You didn't want to listen to State Funeral FM, you wanted the blinkin' weather forecast. But, you're not going to break your principle of Safety First. So you keep your eyes on the road and blindly jab at a few more buttons and get Magic FM, followed by Mellow FM, followed by Nearly

Bleedin' Comatose FM. Then you inadvertently turn the treble up to maximum and the bass down to minimum. When you finally get the station you want the weather item is long since past – and by now a new weather system will have moved in anyway, casting "spits and spots" of rain right where you don't need it.

(On a separate Grump aside; is it just the weather people who use this term? Is it still the legacy of Bill Giles to try and get the nation to adopt the term? We Brits love our weather forecasting abilities, but in casual conversation nobody ever says to me, "We were planning on having a barbecue but I'll have to watch out for a few spits and spots of rain later on." Spits and spots is the lazy-arsed way of saying "We don't know if it's going to rain or not, but we're going to cover our options by saying 'spits and spots'.")

Grump's Law of Car Radios

Only one of the pre-set stations on your car radio will be worth listening to, and at least two will be badly tuned.

RDS

The purpose of the RDS (Radio Data System) installed on your car radio is to allow traffic bulletins to interrupt whatever programme you're listening to. Thus you can be listening to an intensely serious programme, like Radio 4's *From Our Own Correspondent* when some chuckly self-lobotomised arse from Radio Wurzel comes on with, "and what's the news on the roads, Jan?"

"Well we've got an overheated van blockin' up Trowbridge Hoigh Street. The traffic loight on the Bath Road's havin' a bit of a 'mare, keep well clear of that I would, and Farmer Bob sez he's got the comboine out for the first toime this summer and he don't 'ave third gear no more so watch yourself up Three Beggars' Hill after foive. Keep safe out there lovers."

Which is fine – that information will benefit somebody, even if it's nothing you need to be worried about. But then they don't turn the RDS signal off and you have to listen to the next three minutes of Radio Wurzel's drivetime show, which by comparison makes the traffic report seem articulate and entertaining.

What RDS Should Really Do

What I need is the kind of RDS that switches my radio automatically to another station when it hears certain sounds or certain key words. I'm sure this must be possible. My son is constantly going on about his iPhone "Apps" and there's even one called Shazam that can recognize any tune within microseconds of it being played into the microphone. The iPhone is a very impressive bit of kit actually. I'd like it a bit more if my son hadn't formed a permanent relationship with his to the exclusion of all school work.

But I digress. Radio manufacturers need to grab hold of this technology and apply it to car radios. I would want my car radio to re-tune on hearing any of the following:

The Archers, Chris Moyles, Sarah Kennedy, Nigel Kennedy, trad jazz, free jazz, swing jazz, big band jazz, latin jazz, jazz funk, *In Our Time* with Melvyn Bragg, Bob Crow, Mahmoud Ahmadinejad and Alastair Campbell.

F1 Gear Shifts

Want to think that your car is like Lewis Hamilton's or Jenson Button's? Then why not get a car with a paddle gearshift; little levers that change gear located just underneath the steering wheel. They give you that full-on F1 experience. There you are in your SEAT León – the

Fernando Alonso of your road, a regular babe-magnet with your F1 gearshift...

Oh, do me a favour! The SEAT León is as close to resembling an F1 car as Ann Widdecombe is to Elle Macpherson. The reason that F1 gear shifts were developed on the steering wheel was so that drivers didn't need to take their hands off the steering wheel because of the incredible G-forces generated in turns and braking zones. You could steer a SEAT León with your knees round most bends without getting into much trouble. Maybe they have a role on high-performance sports cars that are occasionally used in racing, but on the school run? I don't think so. They are a bit like the rear spoiler, one more thing to go wrong or drop off your car.

If you really want a simulated F1 experience, break down after five minutes of motoring and then bitch that the guy next door to you gets better treatment.

6 CD Changer

I have a device in my car that is nominally a 6 CD player. In practice it's more of a CD warmer, keeping them all toasty and dust-free; a task it performs with a certain minimal level of competence. But, ask it to step outside its comfort zone and actually play any of the six CDs? You get a very teenage response. It might, it might not, it just depends how it's feeling. After a bit of a stand-off, when you ask for one of the CDs back, it goes into a mood and won't. It just won't. That is until you press the button enough times so that it gets fed up and finally offers the CD up with a shrug: "there you are then".

Some CDs it will play first time. Some it keeps forever, and so to some degree it's like a CD piggy bank. I have learnt only to trust it with expendable CDs and long for the day I can get a radio with an MP3 player and it can go **** itself.

Seat Warmers

Amongst the most useless bit of unnecessary junk added to any car is the seat warmer; the device that gives you the uncomfortable feeling you're basking in someone else's arse radiation. I am not part of that constituency that sits down in a chair and goes, "Ooh, nice warm seat." I'm one who grimaces and says, "So who was sitting there, then?"

It's a fleeting advantage. Unless you've got a polar bear's or a penguin's backside, the seat warmer gives you about 20 seconds of warmth before your own in-built radiation takes over and heats the area.

It's probably the only bit of the car that you can be relied upon to warm up yourself and someone's installed a device to do it for you. And if you're blessed with a generously warm arse already, then adding more heat to the situation could end up with some kind of seat-melting inferno.

What would be far more useful is a steering-wheel warmer. Correct me if I'm wrong but in winter it's not your bottom you use to scrape ice off the windows on a frosty morning, it's your hands. Jump into the car having just scraped ice off the windows and a nice warm steering wheel would go a long way to dealing with the bone-penetrating cold. Your arse can look after itself.

Emergency Spare Wheel

What in God's holy firmament were car manufacturers thinking of when they gave us the emergency spare wheel? Let's rewind the tape and go back to that management meeting when it was first proposed by Management Toady:

Toady: I've got a great idea for cutting cost.

Boss: Let's hear it then, I'm all for cutting costs.

Toady: How about instead of manufacturing a proper wheel with a proper spare tyre for our cars, let's save £25 by giving motorists an "emergency spare wheel".

Boss: What's an emergency spare wheel when it's at home?

Toady: It's a tiny cheap tyre on a wheel made out of fourth-rate steel.

Boss: Won't it make the cars look a bunch of crap when it's fitted?

Toady: Yes, but the first time the motorist will see it is probably going to be two years after they bought the car. Not our responsibility.

Boss: And it'll save us £25?

Toady: Maybe £27.50.

Boss: Do you smoke cigars?

You'd think, after you lashed out £17,000 on a brand-new motor, that the first time you had a puncture the replacement wheel wouldn't look like something you got from the scrapyard or the motorist's £1 shop. What's more, when cars have proper replacement wheels, you can just leave that wheel on the car and get the old one repaired. This way round you have to get it repaired, then stick it back on the car and put the emergency spare wheel back in its slot. (Because it mustn't be driven for more than 50 miles or it'll self-destruct.)

Seatbelt Alarms

It's the nanny state in your car – the seatbelt alarm is designed to be as irritating as a small child jabbing you in the leg with a sharpened ice-cream stick – and it works. Rather than listen to that repeated noise, it's much easier to give in and give it what it wants – a good buckling.

Other devices in the car aimed at getting your attention do it in a far more understated way. If you've failed to close the boot, a simple dashboard light alerts you to the fact. If you've left your lights on and then try and open the car door, a small chime rings out. It's a friendly reminder not a hectoring, relentless mallet to the head. Bing, bing, bing, bing, bing!

Seatbelt alarms, given the chance, would probably want to go and report you for speeding or parking on a double yellow line, or using a mobile phone when you shouldn't. They're ready to form an allegiance with a lot of other devices in your car that don't trust you to do the right thing at the right time. Such as the lights, that switch themselves on when it's dark, and the windscreen wipers, that start the moment the windscreen gets wet.

You'd better watch out when the speedo gets the hump and starts talking to the SatNav. Before you know it, the seatbelt alarm will have muscled in there for a piece of the action and the second you go 31 mph it'll be: Bing, bing, bing, bing, bing, bing!

Actually, come to think of it, my SatNav does that already…

Warm-Air Fans

Considering we've had over 110 years of car design, you'd think that by now someone would have worked out how to design a car-heating system that sends heat where you want it. I can choose any of the four settings on the dial of my car and the air goes to exactly the same place every time. Maybe if I choose the windscreen option, a little of it is deflected up there, but never enough to trouble the condensation that builds up like it was the inside of an arctic conservatory with four kettles boiling away inside of it. Although car manufacturers anticipate that the back seats of cars will be used, any attempts to keep them warm have been avoided. To stop rear-seat passengers from constant whingeing you have to set the temperature at the front like it was a sauna in an old people's home.

CHALLENGING JOURNEYS

Mother-in-Law on Board

Contrary to what you might think I am about to write, having the mother-in-law in the car can be a very pleasant experience. For a start she's used to driving with the wife's father, who is a cross between the Monty Python character Arthur Pewty and the Donald Duck cartoon where Donald starts off as a mild-mannered duck and then transmogrifies into Road Rage Satan.

So, the brisk-yet-considerate, ever-vigilant-but-relaxed driving style of yours truly is a joy to behold. She's like Honor Blackman in the Toyota Avensis advert from some years ago, when the most unlikely couple in the world to buy a Toyota Avensis (i.e. young, beautiful, stylish) give the mother-in-law a lift and she criticises anything and everything until she gets in the back seat of the Avensis. During the journey she remains uncharacteristically silent.

My mother-in-law is the same. Provided the optic of Gordon's gin I have installed over the rear seat has about fifteen measures of gin in it (we estimate one measure per

25 miles is a good rule of thumb), and there is an adequate supply of chilled tonic and several packs of large pistachios, she's happier than an old dear in a Day Care Centre.

The only problems we get are when I forget to take the child lock off the rear window buttons and she can't get the window down quick enough for one of her sub-sonic belches. The car's suspension needs to be set to "sport" mode just to cope with the reverb.

But if the optic jams or she spills her last three measures while singing a rousing chorus of "My Old Man's a Dustman"…then it does become a very challenging journey. You wouldn't believe how far that woman can spit a pistachio.

Heading for the Airport

God knows air travel is stressful enough on its own, but when you factor in a car journey around the M25 to get to the airport, the need for some kind of pre-trip psychotherapy seems a virtual necessity.

Leaving the rigours of negotiating Britain's forever-under-repair road network aside, when you get to the airport, you find that the Long Term Parking is about the same distance from the airport as your house was.

Having been directed to Zone ZZ79, where you're confidently led to believe there are spaces, you find nothing but wall-to-wall cars and three spaces that will just about fit a Smart car because of inconsiderate bastards in 4x4s who can't be bothered to park between the white lines.

When you finally locate a part of the car park where there are spaces, you haul the suitcases to the nearest bus stop only to find that the buses are all passing on an adjacent road and that you have stupidly parked in XY43, which is not technically open.

A dishevelled mess, you finally get to the airport and queue up, only to be asked by Ryan Air if you've brought your own oxygen, because there is a £10 oxygen supplement on all their flights. And toilet paper is 50 pence a sheet.

You queue to check in your luggage, you queue for a passport check, you queue for security and jostle in a queue to get on the flight. But smile, you're on holiday!

Wide Margin of Error

The answer to all of this last-minute panic is to leave yourself a big margin of error. Your flight is at 1 p.m. Here's what to do: allow two hours for check-in, half an hour to get parked, one hour for the trip, one hour for safety, plus one hour on top of that to be super-safe. What happens?

The motorway is surprisingly clear and you get there so early that they're not even checking in baggage and you have to hang around with your suitcases looking at airport monitors. When the check-in desk opens you're at the front of the queue and you breeze through passport control and security checks. You get to the other side three and a half hours before your flight is due to be called and your bored children stare at you with hostility, asking why you had to come so early. And then the flight's delayed.

Grump's First Law of Airport Journeys

Delays on journeys to the airport will be proportionately double your degree of lateness. Thus, if you're ten minutes late already, you will be delayed by a further twenty minutes. If you are twenty minutes late, you will be delayed by forty minutes and so on. Up to a maximum of eight hours.

Grump's Second Law of Airport Journeys

If you incur any kind of road traffic offence in order to get to the airport on time – such as jumping a light, or being flashed by a speed camera – then when you get to the airport you'll find your flight is delayed.

Finding the Car in the Long Term

Airport journeys aren't just stressful on the way there. The result of blind panic to get your flight on time can have consequences two weeks later.

You dropped the car in a hurry in the Long Term car park, mid-afternoon, in daylight, and because you were busy making sure you rounded up all the hand baggage, you didn't bother to note the zone down – "It was A-something or other." You noticed the configuration of bus-stops, you'll just go back to A and then you'll remember it.

Two weeks, a rash and many jugs of sangria later, after a long journey, at midnight, the bus drops you back at A-something and you're suddenly struck by the thought that modern cars all look alike. Especially in darkness.

You patrol up and down A-something for half an hour from 01 to 99. Nothing. That maroon-coloured BMW X5 that you parked next to, where's that gone then?

After an hour's fruitless search you actually begin to doubt that you ever left it in A-something, because thinking about it, it could have been B-something. You eventually find your car in Z-99, in the next row across from where you first started looking, and your wife gives you the kind of look that says she is going to start searching for another man the second she gets home and can start browsing Match.com.

Funerals

"He'll be late for his own funeral" is one of those phrases beloved of the older generation. But being late for a funeral is quite an easy proposition, given the tight timetable and the in-out nature of most modern crematoriums.

When a distant cousin died on the golf course I felt obliged to attend. We had to drive to some god-forsaken crematorium in a place I think it is politic not to name (in Kent). Five miles from our destination – feeling pleased that we were half an hour early – we ran into some gas main repairs that had gathered a mile-long queue, which was nicely supplemented by vehicles joining from sideroads.

There was no way out. We had to sit there and grind our teeth till we were through the lights, after which I became Ari Vatanen and Stig Blomqvist in my rallying attempt to get to the place on time. Parking the car backwards with a screech of gravel, we legged it to the crematorium building just as the doors were closing for the short ceremony. It was a plain, but dignified service and being the last ones in we sat at the back looking suitably grave and hoping nobody had noticed how late we were.

It was only when they read the guy's name out that we realised we'd made it to the funeral in front of my cousin's, which had been delayed because of the same road works. So, two funerals in a day.

Euro Tunnel

Taking the train underneath the Channel is easily the quickest option if you want to get to France in a hurry. It's a straightforward process. You queue in lanes before being routed onto a flatbed goods train. You drive on in a big queue, then they shut the divider doors to seal off individual carriages. You're off. The biggest problem is finding anything interesting to look at out of the window or locating a toilet. What's even better, French fisherman have no way of stopping it.

The two occasions we've used it there's been no trouble travelling from England to France. However, on both return journeys it's been anarchy in the car park in Boulogne, resulting in several hours' delay and nasty frayed tempers. How can they cock up something so simple? Even the guys at Stalag Luft III could get people down their tunnels quicker than Euro Tunnel, and they had goons in watch towers armed with machine guns.

Ferry Journeys

Aaah, but there's still a romance to ferry journeys. Plymouth to Roscoff, Portsmouth to Le Havre, Poole to Cherbourg, Dover to Dunkirk, Woolwich to North Woolwich. Coming home from Calais in the early morning, no matter how many Polish builders and their families are sprawled out on the levels below, you can still go out on deck and sniff the salty air as you approach Dover and hear the evocative cries of wheeling gulls above the cliffs.

Cross-Channel ferries may not be the standard bearers of international cuisine, but the whole thing is over in a couple of hours and you can do what you like after that. The complications only come on the longer routes when you have five or six hours to kill.

Generally speaking, the further a ferry has to go, the more tightly packed your car is going to be when you park it on the loading deck. Which means if you're heading off to Spain from Portsmouth, then the ferry company is going to make every last centimetre count. You'll have to nudge up to the car in front and squeeze close to the car at your side, leaving the most ridiculously small gap to open your car door in. As a nation we don't like to scrape each other's paintwork, and as we're not all Mr Wafer, extricating ourselves from the carefully orchestrated gridlock can be a ligament-straining exercise. Sardines have quite a bit of room to stretch out compared to the space they give you on some cross-Channel ferries.

Once on board *The Pride of Ventnor* or *Le Fromage de la Mer* (depending on whether it's P&O or Brittany Ferries), you have to run the gauntlet of French, Spanish, English and American school parties whose soul objective is to run round the boat shrieking in what seems like a five-hour relay race.

Grump's First Law of Overnight Ferry Journeys

If you're on an overnight ferry journey and need to get off the boat rapidly the following morning, watch out for the the person in the car in front of you. They will oversleep and your line of cars will not move until they stumble blearily, and really not very apologetically, onto the car deck. By this time, the last of the trucks will be leaving.

Christenings – The Newquay-to-Barnstaple space / time continuum

I don't want to over-egg this pudding, but in the days before SatNav you were utterly reliant on your distance/time estimating abilities. These days it's a piece of proverbial piddle: you pump in your location, pump your destination in and the device gives you an uncannily accurate idea of how long it will take you to drive from Point A to Point B, observing the speed limits along the way. Back in the day, you had to stare at a map pretty hard.

Now let me ask you this. If it takes just over four hours to drive from London to Newquay, how long do you think it would take you to drive up the coast from Newquay to Barnstaple? Two bloody hours, that's what!

It wouldn't have mattered but we were attending a christening and one of us was an intended god parent.

On that journey, I swear that time evaporated somewhere on the Cornwall/Devon border. Or maybe we passed through one of those time holes that dinosaurs are always popping out of in *Primeval*. We had allowed an hour and fifteen minutes to get there and, before we knew it, the service was already started and we were still ploughing through Devon lanes, miles away.

The Church of England may be a bit more enlightened these days but it still doesn't allow god parents to confirm their duties and obligations over a mobile phone. It's no good yelling, "I turn to Christ" into your Nokia because the vicar's not going to be interested. As a matter of fact, I had already sought Christ Almighty's help with a caravan dawdling along at 20 mph and he hadn't intervened in the slightest.

Bank Holidays

Feast or famine, that's what you get on bank holidays. It's either unseasonably cold, with the vestiges of an Atlantic hurricane ripping through the branches of trees from Porth to Perth (in which case you'll have no traffic on the roads because it's so unmentionably shite out there), or it's unfeasibly warm and sunny (in which case the world and his wife will bung the windbreak in the car and clog up the major coast-bound arteries and reduce the M23 to three crawler lanes, plus a hard shoulder for expired radiators, before you can say, "and a high of 28 degrees").

But Usually it's Foul.

Richard Dawkins may have several arguments about natural selection to chuck at religious fundamentalists but I've got one equally as compelling for those who believe in their "special friend". If God truly loves us, why does he send such crap weather for bank holidays? We've been patient, we've done our time in the wilderness and we don't need sub-zero temperatures to "try" us – we have the *Eurovision Song Contest* and video remote controllers for that.

And if he does care to orchestrate a spell of high pressure over the British Isles for the weekend what he could also do is make sure the major road schemes have all the cones neatly put away from the middle of Friday afternoon. It's not too much to ask from a deity, is it?

Minicabs

Listen: isn't that the sound of Mellow MagicFM featuring the best of Phil Collins, The Corrs and Lighthouse Family? Sniff: isn't that the exotic smell of a traffic-lights air freshener mingled with take-away curry jammed into the interior trim in 2004? Feel: isn't that the weary sag of six-year-old velour seating? Well then, we must be in the back of a minicab.

There's an unwritten rule amongst minicab drivers that you are not allowed to use a car that has under 150,000 miles on the clock or any of the original body panels. They are cars that have already lived a full life and are clinging on gamely to their mechanical functions till the next service is due.

What is absolutely astounding, is just how many of them are out there. When they started introducing those rear windscreen stickers in the London area a few years ago, it was like the sudden realisation moment in a zombie movie. You had the feeling something strange was going on but then, Zoiks!, you looked all around at the traffic lights and you were surrounded by minicabs – driven by zombies. In London, it's estimated that 80 per cent of the cars on the road on a Friday night are minicabs. And the rest are just parents providing that role for their party-loving children in cars totally unfit for that role (i.e. roadworthy, clean and odour-free).

There's a residual grubby feel to minicabs that brings out my Howard Hughes side. Get into the back of one and you immediately start thinking of contracting the Noro Virus, Swine Flu or Legionnaire's Disease. Mercifully, the drivers rarely engage you in conversation and you can devote your time to figuring out if it's the exhaust that's rattling or he's trailing a line of tins behind the car, the kind the best man attaches to the bride and groom's car.

Incidentally, we once went to a wedding where the bridegroom's college friends – unknown to the minicab driver – tied a large metal dustbin to the bumper that the happy couple were about to go away in. The bride and groom emerged in their going away outfits to say all their goodbyes, thank-yous and extended kissy farewells which was a bit of a peeve for the driver who was on a fixed fare. So when it was time to leave he took off at a fair old lick...followed 30 metres later by the dustbin making one hell of a clank. The noise must have spooked the driver because all of sudden he slammed on his brakes, only to find a large metal dustbin crashing into the back of his car at 30 mph a few seconds later. That was a funny wedding.

The Minicab as a Hotel

Incidentally, if you're ever travelling to the continent and are lured in by one of those "Formule 1" cheap-and-cheerful hotels, be warned. They are the minicab equivalent of a proper hotel. Stepping into one of their bedrooms is like taking a ride in an eight-year-old Toyota Camry driven by a reformed smoker. The only place in the world for carpet tiles is the foyer of Speedy Fit. I'm pretty certain that they're called F1 hotels because people want to get out of them at top speed.

Black Cab Drivers

Popular mythology has it that they won't go south of the river, can't stop talking, can't *start* listening, are forever picking up minor celebrities and have politics to the right of Genghis Khan. Which all sounds reasonably accurate.

To earn a cabby's licence they have to pass a rigorous test known as "The Knowledge", which tests their ability to navigate across London from one given street to another. There are also tests to find out how much they know about East End history, the Kray Twins, Pearly Kings and Queens, plus where you can still buy pie and mash. Owing to an administrative error, only the area of South London from Blackfriars Bridge to Waterloo Bridge was included in the South London section of The Knowledge. This allows cabbies to drop fares at Waterloo Station, the National Theatre, the Southbank Centre and the London Eye. Beyond that is a large area of swamp until you get to Dulwich or Greenwich, which is outside the distance a cabby is obliged to take you.

There is strict dress code of Farah slacks and Pringle jumpers, white socks and Italian loafers. Plus the occasional nice bit of chunky jewellery. It used to be a sovereign ring, but that's a bit old-school now. Black cab drivers are obliged to post an out-of-focus photo of their family, or wife, somewhere on the dashboard of their cab. If only to remind them to stay out later and pick up that one last fare rather than go home and have to sit through the latest Jordan exclusive on Living TV with the missus.

PARKING

Multi-Story Car Parks – Depressing or Uplifting?

Your heart never lifts when you enter a multi-story car park, does it? There is never a little skip of joy as you wonder which particular level will have a space for you today. Will it be an inward-facing slot on Level 4, or an outward slot on Level 7, or perhaps a corner slot on Level 11? They are a place of necessity, often frustration and at times unmitigated misery.

I have a recurrent nightmare that I am stuck forever in a car park, and you can be assured it's not a bark-floored, tree-lined Forestry Commission car park out in the wilds of Northumberland.

Multi-story car parks are popular spots for suicides. This is no great surprise, as being in one doesn't particularly make you want to cling onto this world for much longer. Unless you're a big fan of Tate Modern, in which case you might be enthralled by the formal and monolithic brutalism of the concrete structure and the nihilistic sentimentalism of the use of grey. Why a multi-story car park has failed to win the Turner Prize is beyond me, they are the places you might least associate with creative artistic expression and hence by absurdist logic, the it-can't-be-art-so-it-obviously-is-art reasoning kicks in. Has Rachel Whiteread done a multi-story? I suppose it's only a matter of time. Then you'll get a lot of poncey art critics flocking to it, there'll be a piece on Channel 4 News and Melvyn Bragg will do a Southbank Show on it five years after it has become untrendy.

Had A.A. Milne lived long enough to build a multi-story car park in the most beautiful corner of the 100 Acre Wood, then Eeyore would have been at home in there. Forget all the stuff about Eeyore's Gloomy Place, he'd be straight under that barrier and doing a little dance like Piglet. There's an element of Eeyore in every car park attendant you ever meet.

Apart from depressing the bejesus out of you, multi-story car parks are also dangerous places. Casual muggings aside, spend any length of time in one after dark and you'll find your way into a suspend-your-disbelief-BBC-spy-caper, a Let's-work-backwards-from-the-body crime drama or a maverick cop romp. It's such lazy cinematic shorthand now. The second the camera cuts to the hero striding towards his car under that stark neon strip lighting, jangling his car keys, you know an incident is about to take place. The wife never pops out from behind the bonnet with a bunch of friends and a celebration cake from M&S. No, there's a confrontation, a threat, a menace, an assault just about to happen.

If they parked in an open-air car park they'd be safe. Nobody ever draws alongside and gives you your final warning in a darkened car park. It's too difficult to see the carefully contrived menacing expression. There's a strict rule: multi-stories are for threats and kidnapping, darkened car parks are for disposing of the body.

Multi-Storys with Squeaky Floors

Yer posh integrated multi-story is a high-end variation of the car park. They're normally attached to brand-new stores like John Lewis or Waitrose, whose customers expect a different kind of parking misery.

You know you're in one of these the minute you step out of the car, because they've illuminated the place properly and painted the floor like it was a car dealer's showroom.

Actually, you know you're in one a lot earlier than that because the squealing sound of the tyres on the painted surface makes you sound like you're in a chase sequence from *The Sweeney* when you're doing about 5 mph. This makes doddery Honda Accord drivers slow down from their natural cruising speed of 7 mph to about 3 mph. In fact, Honda Accord drivers are so slow that they need to budget for a service interval in between entering a multi-story car park and finally pulling the handbrake on. Many die from malnutrition while parking each year.

Barrier Panics

Part of the multi-story experience is "barrier panic syndrome". This is categorised as, "The fear of getting to the only exit barrier of a large multi-story car park, sticking your ticket in, only to find out you haven't paid." The queue of vehicles that mounts up behind gets more and more irate as their timed tickets are all slowly running out while your car obstructs the exit. Tempers fray as quickly as an Asda bag with more than four items.

Sometimes it produces drastic consequences. We were exiting a car park in Hemel Hempstead and the barrier sequence was quite clear: place ticket in, barrier goes up, car leaves, barrier goes down again and so on. Only our ticket seemed to aggravate the machine and it was spat straight out like a toddler rejecting an unloved vanilla dessert. I turned it round, it spat it out again. I tried it upside down. No joy. We'd validated the ticket and driven straight to the exit, so there couldn't be a problem. There was no other alternative than to "press for assistance". While the exit-machine man was scrambled, I indicated that it was the machine's fault by the universal mime of shrugging and holding my hands palm upwards. In the rear-view mirror I could see tension was rising in the car behind, but her ticket wasn't going to work either so my conscience was clear.

When the man came down to try my ticket he told me, fairly tight-lipped, that I'd sat on it and creased it and that's why it wouldn't work. It looked like a faint crease, yes, but I wasn't going to argue. By this time I'd gathered an impressive exit tail of about 40 vehicles, all jostling for position in various exit queue tributaries; a rising tide of malcontents all anxious to breathe the cleaner air outside.

He slipped a credit card into the slot and the barrier rose up, releasing us into the Saturday traffic. But the excitement wasn't over. The car behind had forgotten the sequence and tried to follow us through. As the barrier came down there was a hideous crumping sound as the machinery got wrenched off its mountings and a scene of carnage unfolded in the rear-view mirror. But we were all right, we were out.

Multi-Story Loiterers

On my list of despicable people, and not far above child molesters and TV chefs, is the multi-story car park loiterer. We've all seen them. These are the people who, upon entering a busy multi-story car park, instead of driving safely and swiftly to the level where there are lots of free spaces, insist on securing the space closest to the ground floor. So they creep along from floor to floor, making sure that every last space in every last row is occupied, before creeping slowly up to the next level and repeating the process.

They neither think nor care about the train of vehicles crawling along behind them, who would be quite happy to go up another three levels and walk the extra 24 steps down. It's impossible to overtake these motoring wildebeests in such narrow confines, especially when they've placed their Nissan Micra slap bang in the centre of the lane, you just have to sit behind and watch your life ebb slowly away.

These very same people, upon spotting someone returning to their car with shopping, go into a frenzy, jam on the brakes and bring the pursuing crocodile to a standstill. They wait while all the shopping is loaded, the children have been belted in and the car reversed out before taking five minutes to manoeuvre into the vacated space. One level up there are a dozen free places, but no, this one was technically closer.

Death cannot come too soon for the multi-story loiterer. In the Grump Republic there would be a shadowy ministry – the Secretariat of Motoring Correction – who would remove Multi-Story Loiterers from the population and take them away for "retraining" and they would never be seen again. My only pleasure in a multi-story car park is to return to the car with conspicuous shopping bags, attracting the immediate attentions of a Loiterer. When I know I've suckered her in, I make sure I load them very slowly and carefully, often changing my mind where they should go – boot or backseat, it's a conundrum. Then I open the driver's door for a rummage. Rummage. After a fruitless rummage I shut the door, and continue shopping. Should I be asked the question, "Are you going?" I reply, "Yes." Then I lock the car and go.

Parking Ticket Machines

Parking ticket machines are like donkeys, they're never happy on their own. When they have a whole car park to cater for they get withdrawn, become moody and break down. This forces you to scrabble around in the car for a pen and a scrap of paper and jam a hastily written note to place on the dashboard.

Two minutes after you have left the car park two men arrive in a van, one repairs the machine and the other goes round the car park issuing tickets to everyone who's got a hastily written note.

One ticket machine on its own will have days when it refuses to recognise any change that is legal tender. No matter how much spin you put on your seemingly identical pound coin. Put two ticket machines (or more) in a car park together and they'll be fine. They'll print out tickets all day long, issue change, not be fazed by foreign currency or even some bastard sticking coins in with double-sided tape (see Parking Meters). Two ticket machines together couldn't be happier and three are happier still, but as Three Dog Night told us all those years ago, "One is the Loneliest Number".

Parking Charges

You don't need to be Mary Portas – Mary Queen of Strops – to work out why sales on the Internet are growing. Is it any surprise when the cost of parking your car for three hours in the city centre of a Saturday could feed a family for a week (provided they shopped at Lidl)? Shopping is a hateful experience and Christmas shopping is the apogee of all that is bad in the "experience" – inflated prices, crowds, queues, awful weather, badly sung carols, unlimited Slade and parking charges.

Rip-off Britain ensures that you have to pay for what you don't need, so if you want to shop for an hour and ten minutes you have to pay for two hours. Some unscrupulous operators arrange the time increments so that you are forced to pay way more than you need: one hour, two hours, six hours and four years. Unlike all the high-street shops, car parks don't have sales. So while property prices have nose-dived, clothes shops slashed their margins and electronic retailers gone bust – car parks, like state sector pensions, pretend it's all not happening.

There is an argument that for those who view shopping as an enjoyable leisure activity it's reasonable value for money – a film that lasts a couple of hours will probably cost you a tenner once you've made the downpayment on a hopper of popcorn. It might turn out to be a crap film and you didn't realise it was directed by Lars von Trier (though the plot line, of septuagenarian ex-porn star slays toy boys with range of power tools, might have been the giveaway). So, as a facilitator of the free activity of shopping, parking charges could be viewed as the ticket of admission. But if you are obliged to pay for retail torture, not therapy, they're crap.

Parking Meters

Gone are the days when you could just rock up to a spot in central London, park the car, jam a couple of fifty pence pieces in the meter, see a top show, then go off for a luxury meal at Garfunkels restaurant.

Hyper-inflation of parking charges has meant that you need enough spare change to stock a slot machine to park the car for more than an hour and a half. First parking meters went digital, then the London boroughs realised they could dispense with them altogether, in particular, the blokes they sent round to empty them out. Instead of paying the high fixed costs of maintaining a meter and replacing it once in a while, they could switch to a pay-by-phone process and employ extra parking assistants to a) check that money was being paid and b) whack parking tickets on anybody else they should encounter.

These days, if you want to drop your car into a central London parking bay you need to set-up a parking account with credit card details, phone or text through your Bay Number, the length of time you want to be parked for, plus information on the shoes you'll be wearing, the purpose of your visit and your mother's maiden name.

And because you don't have to find the physical cash – it's all going onto a credit card – then you're suckered into paying even more for the vastly over-priced privilege. The champions of the scheme extol the virtues of its flexibility. If you're running late, you can simply ring up again from wherever you are and top-up your time, thus preventing a needless journey back to the car. My friends, that is the tip of the iceberg of a descent into moral decay. Our country didn't become great by not having the discipline to get back to the car for a certain time. That is why we ended up with a credit crunch.

The whole pay-by-phone system falls to pieces when you park and find that your mobile phone is low on battery and flatlines in the middle of your phone call, text or SMS. Or you can't get through, or you can't get a signal, or you forgot it, or it's a pay-as-you-go and your credit runs out…

Parking by phone has put an end to that dying art – the deliberately jammed meter. "Stone me, Gov, it was like that when I parked here." Careful experimentation with an array of 10 pence pieces and increasing layers of double-sided tape wrapped around them had produced the perfect jamming thickness…for a friend of mine. One such 10 pence piece, suitably clad, would give a day's free parking – provided you didn't get greedy and do it more than once a week.

Parking Blockheads

Thanks to that hardy band of souls the driving test inspectors, the standard of roadcraft in this country is pretty good. "What?" I hear you say, as your jaw hangs open. "Has Grump gone soft in the head and become the Sir David Attenborough of the highway?", a man with rarely a cross word for anyone.

But no, it's true. The standard of driving in the UK for people who passed their test in the last 40 years is remarkably high. Yes, you do get the odd coffin-dodger who thinks that their judgement hasn't changed, even though their hips have long since gone to meet their maker, but generally the driving is good. It's the parking that's absolute crap.

People who seem perfectly sane when they're driving along, capable of rational thought and kind deeds, lose all judgement when they become stationary.

Fussy Parkers

There's a small band of motorists who believe that parking is like a dressage event, the Olympic discipline of horsey manners. None of them go to the extent of dressing up like they were in a Jane Austen novel and going over to see Mr Bingley (whose balls are divine) but they do take positioning their car very seriously. The object of the task is to place the vehicle precisely between the two white lines of a parking space with equal gaps either side and with the car's sides perfectly parallel.

Fussy parkers believe in the power of feng shui and the benefits of all the chi energy which flows from flawless alignment. They will manoeuvre backwards and forwards and backwards and forwards in an inexorable bid to get their cars straight with slide-rule accuracy.

Even if they've only nipped down to the newsagent for a paper they will not skimp on their quest. Each and every parking move must be completed with Jedi-like intensity and a bid for geometric harmony.

Novice parkers will open their car doors mid-park for a bit of extra guidance, but the beauty of the art is in the purity of judgement which each driver bestows upon their parking position. The zen master fussy parker will not countenance a sneaky look while they position their vehicle. They must use light and stars and gravity and experience.

They may be spiritually fulfilled by the parking experience but in practice that doesn't stop them being judgemental about other people's efforts. I have a rich insight into the mindset of a fussy parker because I'm married to one and I'm constantly being given a critique of other vehicles. It's the same kind of mentality that searches out misplaced apostrophes in school newsletters and reports them to the school with unsuppressed glee.

Approximate Parkers

Approximate Parkers don't care where they park the car as long as it's stopped and the handbrake's on. They are the ying to the Fussy Parkers' yang. Reversing into a space between two vehicles is a real chore for them so as long as it's three-quarters in, then for them it's job done. No need to straighten up, they'll be gone in an hour or so and what will it matter…?

Like Scalextric Man (who we'll meet later), they are afraid of the kerb and anything to their left, thus you could possibly play a decent game of football in the gap they leave between themselves and the pavement.

The best example of an Approximate Parker was a friend of our elderly Scottish neighbour who we'll name, "my dear friend Mary". Apart from the fact that she drove an Austin Maestro (the kind of car that crushers were invented for), she had only a vague notion of parking. When she parked – and I use the term loosely – it was difficult to know if she had been driving along and just stopped, or if she had made a concerted attempt to get nearer to the kerb.

My wife, who as you know, is not the most patient of women, was angered at first. Later she got into the spirit of things by taking photos every time she came round so we could compare "my dear friend Mary's" best efforts to date. When she stopped popping over we asked Mrs MacLeod what had happened. "She got hit by a fire engine, dear" was the reply. We knew why.

45

Women in 4x4s

Heaven knows, I'm the last person in the world you could accuse of being sexist, but what is it about stupid blonde women parking big 4x4s? Men have numerous faults, I grant you. Two tasks at once is one task too many for men whereas women can multi-task till the cows come home. They can bitch about that woman from school, while ordering a cappuccino whilst giving themselves a self-pedicure, no trouble at all. Parking reasonably sized cars is not difficult for a lot of women, but ask them to park a 4x4 or manoeuvre an MPV and it's like you've handed them the keys to an articulated tank transporter.

Car manufacturers have got wise to this and installed parking aids to the front and back bumpers so that women have an audible as well as a visual clue as to when they're going to hit something. The device beeps at you and the beeping gets quicker and quicker as the object behind gets closer and closer. They particularly appeal to women because they make parking sound like a really dramatic episode of *ER*. I fully anticipate the day when 4x4s will come equipped with forward- and side-scanning radar, so that all you have to do is get the vehicle into the approximate position it needs to go and let a computerised parking aid do the rest. A Stepford car for a Stepford wife.

Drive Encroachers

An Englishman's home is his castle, a Welshman's home is his caer, a Scotsman's home is his tower house and an Irishman's home is his dun – and you better not park in front of any of them. It is the inalienable right of a citizen to have free access to the public highway 24/7 and anyone who should choose to nudge a bumper or front wing in front of their driveway is asking for that bumper to be hacked off by a mob of Grump-backed driveway vigilantes exacting Grumpia Law.

All right, a few centimetres isn't going to hurt anyone, it's when some unthinking bastard parks close enough to your line-of-exit to make reversing out awkward or hazardous.

I'm not one of those house owners who curtain-twitch the minute anyone parks outside of my house (I've got the warning signs, the cones and the mock gibbet in the front garden for that). It's the lazy-arsed casualness of not finding a proper-size parking space that annoys me. A Drive Encroacher can't be bothered to park his car properly – "that'll do," is his motto. It's the selfish "me, me, me" attitude that really gets my goat and, as you can ascertain from some of the blunt-speaking on these pages, my goat's not that accessible.

Along with Multi-Story Loiterers, the Driveway Encroacher would be dealt with severely in the Grump Republic, as would the Drive Blocker. "I'm just picking something up, mate, won't be two minutes!" Yeah, right.

47

Sundry Parking Bastards

Bumper kissers – These are the arses who park so close to you that you can't actually stand between your boot and their bonnet without losing the blood supply to your ankles. It is a fundamental human right to be able to stand behind your car. If someone does this to you I recommend that you use their front bumper as a kind of step. Test out the step to make sure it's as solid as it should be. Go on, really test it.

Road blockers – Nature abhors a vacuum and a car parked on one side of a narrow road attracts another car to it like a wasp to a jam pot. The tragedy is that the innocent car that parked there first is always the one that gets its wing mirror clipped and broken.

Space Stealers – The standard mode for entering a parking space in the UK is reversing in backwards. This is achieved by driving past the space whilst indicating with the appropriate indicator. Once the road is clear ahead and behind, the driver is free to manoeuvre his vehicle backwards into the space…that's providing some bastard hasn't dived in first. People can see that you've stopped and you're indicating – the only reason you don't reverse is out of courtesy to your fellow road user, who then nicks the space. Under Grumpia Law that would be a right foot gone.

GRUMP'S WORLD OF MOTORSPORT

As the signs around motor racing circuits warn you – motorsport is a dangerous business and it's a leisure activity that involves risk. There's a risk that you might be entertained somewhere along the line.

F1

The glam sport above all glam sports, a Formula One race is a bit like marriage; all the exciting and interesting stuff happens at the start. As it grinds on – seemingly for years – it settles down into a dull routine and gets progressively more boring, with the odd flurry of activity around pit-stops, but otherwise fading out into utter tedium. Nobody overtakes anybody except at the start or unless they have a puncture. Certainly, there is more overtaking in marriage than in F1.

The former president of the sport's governing body, Max Mosley, who was revealed by the *News of the World* to enjoy spanking sessions in a Chelsea basement with five hookers, failed to inject any of that excitement into races. Mosley once defended F1 by saying that it was like an absorbing game of chess with the occasional overtaking moves to be savoured. Which just shows you how out of touch with reality he was – when it comes to televised sport, chess is way up there with air-rifle shooting and bog snorkelling as a must-see event.

Should you want to sit in a grandstand to watch the British Grand Prix, then prepare to pay £300 for the pleasure. That £300 will buy you a seat the size of a small notebook, you'll get wind-tossed, rained on, deafened and have no idea what's going on in the race. The only time you'll know what's going on is when the anoraks all around you groan at Lewis Hamilton's exit or cheer at Jenson Button's success or Fernando Alonso's car breaking down.

F1 Drivers and Insurance Claims

Driving a car at unutterably fast speeds can alter your mental processes. This is clearly evidenced when you get two F1 drivers to explain an accident where one car has rammed into another instead of overtaking it. To the humble observer it looks like one car has shot up the inside at a corner, left it far too late and instead of nipping in front, has slammed into the side of the other car as it turns in. (Gerhard Berger made a career of this.) Interviewed afterwards, the conspicuously guilty driver – far from being apologetic – blames the other driver for a number of reasons, ranging from "I was alongside and he turned in on me," to "He closed the door at the last minute."

The ultimate never-wrong driver was Michael Schumacher. Apart from deliberately crashing into Damon Hill and Jacques Villeneuve while attempting to win World Championships, the Red Baron once produced the limpest of spins at the exit of the Rascasse turn to try and block the track in qualifying for the Monaco Grand Prix. Schumacher had already set the quickest time and with one minute to go was set for pole position, nobody could go quicker than him, if he conveniently left his car in the way…

The faux spin didn't convince anyone. As an F1 excuse it was on a par with "the dog ate my homework, miss". Feeling that they had to back up their driver, the Ferrari team issued a press release along the lines of "the dog was clearly hungry and Michael's homework was very delicious, why shouldn't it get eaten…?"

Unfortunately for Schumacher, this was at the end of his career and he already had "form". The stewards sent him to the back of the grid, though the Ferrari team continued to splutter on about how the dog was for ever eating important paperwork and how outraged they were, no doubt saying "mamma mia!" somewhere along the line. The moral of this tale is, never have an accident with an F1 driver and hope to keep your no-claims bonus, they're all liars.

Touring Car Racing

How to describe? It's a bit like the M25 on a Friday afternoon but more of the vehicles have numbers. Because the cars are very evenly matched, overtaking can be tricky, especially when you consider it's supposed to be a no-contact sport. But like kids in a classroom that have been told not to talk, they can't keep it up for very long.

As the race goes on, there's an increasing amount of whispering, tagging, body rubbing and bumper nudging. Eventually, in the last few laps, it's reduced to no-holds-barred cheating, shunts, sideswipes and reckless lunges, until what's left of the cars crosses the line. This is followed by a big driver punch-up in the car park afterwards – which is usually more interesting than the race that preceded it.

Rallying

You have to question the sanity of anyone who would choose to hurtle down a rutted gravel farm track at speeds of over 100 mph. Sideways. That's what rally drivers like to do and some actually chuckle while doing it. No surprise, then, that many of them come from Finland. Those long, dark winters can affect the soul.

Whereas you and I would have one fist knotted tight and buried in our mouth, heart rate at 180, eyes out like organ stops and eyebrows up where Posh Spice keeps her sunglasses, rally men glance casually at maps as though they were on a Sunday afternoon amble round the Dales.

While the drivers must have balls the size of Buster Gonads', their co-drivers or navigators are the ones with *cahunas major*. At least the driver can see what he's about to hit. The poor old co-driver has to look at his notes, look up, look down again, while being thrown from side to side and bounced about like a supermarket trolley on a flight of steps. A couple of Quells car sickness tablets isn't going to be much help to him. The co-driver has to maintain calm as the madman behind the wheel flings the car to the edge of precipitous mountain roads while simultaneously continuing to bark out obscure commands such as, "Left over crest into short right 4, tightens, don't cut."

The only warning a co-driver gets before the sudden impact with a tree, rock, gatepost or sheep is a dreadful moment when the usually calm driver freezes and draws breath, then it's bang, crash, roll, bang, bang, crash, whummpf, silence.

Le Mans

Over 60,000 Brits regularly attend the Le Mans 24 Hours, but only four people watch the race. After about five laps, when the really fast prototype cars have already lapped the more normal-looking sportscars, you can't tell who's leading who anyway. It's a fast one, it's a slow one, it's a fast one, it's a slow one – you get the picture, like that for another 23 hours and 30 minutes. At which juncture the whole purpose of the Le Mans weekend kicks in (or maybe resumes): the beer-drinking contest.

Married men of a certain getting-away-from-the-wife age use Le Mans as a justification for getting pissed out of their heads on 25cl bottles of Kronenbourg or Pelforth or Heineken. It's an annual male-bonding exercise where the shared task is to build a wall of little bottles bigger than your neighbour's. Inebriation also helps them face up to the dreadful prospect of camping in Northern France with other men who are now a lot older and smellier than when they first went to the Reading Festival together.

The *Guinness Book of World Records* entry for the largest quantity of kebabs ever eaten in one day would surely fall if it were attempted at Le Mans.

The fact that the race is ancillary to the whole getting away and drinking is borne out by hundreds of groups of men straggling back on the cross-Channel ferries from Sunday through to the following Wednesday. Ask anyone who comes back from the race the simple question, "Who won?" and you'll get perplexed shrugs. "I don't know, but I'm pretty sure they were driving an Audi." As the saying goes – if you can remember who won Le Mans, you weren't there, man.

NASCAR

NASCAR is 40 fat blokes called Billy-Bob all driving the same kinds of car painted in different sponsors' colours. They circulate around an oval track in a long line jostling for position and occasionally refuelling or having accidents. This grinds on until the very last lap when the man in fourth place jumps into the lead and wins off the final bend.

NASCAR was a motor sport born in the Confederate south of America, so it's hardly surprising that a fanbase who thought slavery was a good thing finds this entertaining. NASCAR fans don't go to races to see who wins, they go to watch the accidents. Compared to the hardcore accident porn of banger derbies NASCAR is softcore accident porn, with the same kind of intellectual participation.

They have to race on ovals because the attention span of the fans is so small that were the cars to go out of sight for more than ten seconds they'd lose interest and wander off to buy take-away food. NASCAR races won't run in rainy conditions because all the food would get wet.

Drag Racing

Populated by the kind of people you see on *Scrapheap Challenge*, this is an American sport that has caught the imagination of UK fans about as much as baseball and rodeo riding. Practised at the laughably named Santa Pod Raceway, straddling that ol' county line of Bedford County and Northampton County, it's the place where you can see Top Fuel Dragsters, Funny Cars and Ultimate Street Machines. Basically, someone with too much time and a lock-up garage on their hands will have spent two years strapping a Saturn V rocket into an old Fiesta chassis with extra bits welded on, plus the front wheels of a pram to steer it. Stick on a rear spoiler, get some enormous fat-boy tyres and rock up to that Spanish Mission style raceway and let that big ol' freak rip.

Drag Racing is the Sumo wrestling of motorsport, it's all posturing and preparation and waiting around, followed by a frantic 3.4 seconds, after which it's all over. When the lights go out either one competitor explodes, or the clutch breaks, or there's such a difference in reaction to the start lights that the contest's over in the first 70 yards. Should you wish to see what your own transport can do on the Quarter Mile then be sure to attend a "Run What You Brung" meeting. Deploying a parachute after the finish line may not be necessary.

THE LAW

Traffic Policemen

Remember that old saying: "If you can, do. If you can't, teach." To take it a stage further: "If you can, do. If you can't, teach. If you can't teach, become a policeman." And if you have trouble writing things down, become a traffic policeman.

Traffic policemen are genetically still part of *Homo sapiens sapiens*, though at times you could be mistaken for thinking they are closer to *Balanus balanoides*, the common barnacle. They're great at simple mechanical tasks such as directing traffic or clinging onto a rock. Rubbish at anything that involves cognitive thought.

Traffic policemen are the special needs department of the police service. At school, the boys who couldn't get on with books were given a car to take apart and to make them feel less stupid it was called "Applied Science". It's the same with the police service. Those who are semi-literate get to investigate crimes and write reports and appear on *Crimewatch UK*, while those who can only be trusted to fill in the gaps in forms, get a car or a motorbike to play with. In return they have to swear an oath of allegiance to maintain an unflinching desire to apply fixed penalties, no matter what the circumstances.

I used to think that a traffic policemen's anger was affected. How could you be angry at the kind of highway code violation you see every two minutes as you drive into a city centre? They must see that kind of thing all the time when they're off duty and be powerless to do anything about it.

Then the penny dropped. That's why they're so angry. They're making up for lost time.

Grump vs The Sheriff

Whilst commuting by bike I was once chased and stopped by a police motorcyclist. He had been chatting to a lorry driver on the approaches to Hammersmith Bridge. With one side of the road gridlocked and the end of the road taped off, I assumed he was checking that the lorry didn't contain a bomb. Hammersmith Bridge is an easy one to blow up; the IRA have had a couple of goes at it in the past. So, instead of cycling right by him, as though I was trying to earwig his conversation, I detoured the wrong side of a zebra crossing, which was split into two, and cycled towards the bridge to see if it was still accessible to pedestrians.

Bad move. Can you spot what I'd done? Yes, in a completely abnormal traffic situation, with one end of the road closed, I'd cycled the WRONG side of a bollard. Nee nar, nee nar, nee nar, nee nar! "Pull over!"

The police motorcyclist lectured me for ten minutes

then introduced himself as the Sheriff of Barnes. Yeah, right. Not exactly Dodge City is it – Barnes? The lawless town of luvvies where cappuccino rage over a spilled hot drink can lead to a threateningly less than sincere, "Oooh, I'm soooo sorry." Badass Barnes.

But he was right and proper angry that I'd travelled the wrong side of that bollard. At the time I thought what a complete and utter t*t, but in retrospect I realise that he was only doing his job. In Barnes you have to take what crime on the street you can get.

Fun with Fixed Penalties

Excuse the personal reminiscences, but I'm not being paid much to write this book so I see it as a kind of therapy. The policeman who gave me a fixed notice for using a slip-road off the A3 outside of the specified hours was definitely of the rock-clinging, mud-filtering *bivalve* type.

> "Was I aware of the restrictions on the use of this slip road?"
> "Yes."
> "This slip road cannot be used between 7.00 a.m. and 9.30 a.m."
> "I know – it's because the residents further down don't want cars speeding past their houses. That's why I'm parking right here."

"No, actually it's for safety reasons. You can't make a safe turn."

"There wasn't a car behind me when I turned."

"It doesn't matter, it's 8.30 a.m."

"So at 9.30 a.m. it's dangerous and at 9.31 a.m. it suddenly becomes safe, whether you've got a lorry tucked up behind you or not?"

"I don't make the rules and I must let you know I AM going to give you a ticket."

"You're allowed to use your discretion."

"I won't be."

He took my details down and then there's a glorious bit of the Fixed Penalty form where he has to take down a verbatim quote, which I dictated slowly to him. I missed a real opportunity. I should have said slowly and ponderously: "UPON MAKING THE TURN, THE VISION OF AN OWL PEEPING FURTIVELY OVER THE BUSHES AND JUGGLING SEVERAL FIELD MICE DISTRACTED MY ATTENTION", if only to see how much of it he copied down. Alternatively, give him a sentence with some really difficult spellings. Include the words; supersede, caribbean, veterinary, risotto, rhythm, pharaoh and pejorative.

I'm going to write a small improbable statement and keep it in the glove compartment for the next time I make the turn into that sliproad at 8.30 a.m. So at least I can look forward to some fun and games with my next fixed penalty.

Handling the Police

When you're stopped by the police, every fibre of your body might be screaming to tell them to shove their little lectures and homilies up their arses. We don't need the, "Were you aware, sir...?" routine, it's just so much "blah, blah, blah". Where were they when the car behind overtook at 70 mph in a 30 mph zone and clipped your wing mirror? Where were they when the minicab driver didn't see you and pulled out and you flat-spotted a perfectly good set of Dunlops standing on the brakes to avoid him, then watched helplessly as he gave you the middle finger? Eh?

Those were real driving offences, not driving along with one sidelight extinguished, which, with a gentle tap, comes on again.

You want to be as arsey as Victor Meldrew in need of root canal work, but it's an approach that's as useful as sticking your head in a woodworking vice and tightening the handle. And just as difficult to extricate yourself.

When you're stopped by the police you have to be as polite as possible. Whatever you do, DO NOT contradict them on a point of law. They are proud to have remembered what little they can and for you to tell them that it's wrong isn't going to go down well.

Also, bear in mind they will have some right-on politician demanding that any police stops be "proportionate" to the community. It may well be that Porsches, BMWs and TVRs commit the most speeding offences, but that doesn't mean to say that the police should target these vehicles when looking down the barrel of a speed gun on a dual carriageway. Oh no, that would be wholly offensive to all our sensibilities – so to keep the statistics up they have to haul in grannies in Nissan Micras who didn't realise it was a 30 mph restriction and mums on their way to work who got delayed because Cessily didn't want to let go at the day nursery.

HOSTYD – There's Lovely

The reason that traffic policemen are hacked off is probably because they have to remember so many acronyms. Motoring is chock-full of them. The DVLA is of course the place in Swansea where you get your tax disc from and an MOT is what you need to prove your car is just about capable of becoming a minicab when it's on its last legs.

While we're on the subject of acronyms, people marvel when I tell them that the electric company EDF stands for Électricité de France as though I have shared the most incredible secret. Recently they were behind a scheme to make Britain greener by producing less carbon emissions. Well of course they bleedin' would be, they've got massive nuclear reactors sitting across the Channel with over-capacity. Anyway, I digress.

The police have a variety of motoring acronyms and they need to be learned like a 12-times table. I quite like DAI, which stands for Deeper Accident Investigation. This surely suggests that there's some pretty superficial accident investigation going on at the moment and occasionally they make up their minds to bring in DAI. The law also use: RTA (Road Traffic Accident) and RTC (Road Traffic Collision), the difference being what exactly? One was a complete accident and the other was a bit of Michael Schumacher body-panel rubbing to get the last remaining free car park space in Majestic Wine?

HOSTYD, like DAI, sounds Welsh but actually stands for the Hollow Spike Tyre Deflation device, or "Stinger", much loved by programmes such as *Police Camera White-Van Action!*

There's the lovely guttural TWOC (Taking Without Owner's Consent), often also known as THEFT. VASCAR is a bit sci-fi, a bit alien planet, but officially stands for Visual Average Speed Camera and Recorder. Useful for a pub quiz, if nothing else.

In motor racing, Irish driver Eddie Irvine used to be known as "Irv" but in police-speak IRV becomes an Incident Response Vehicle.

However, the acronym I like best is PQMS and it's used across the whole of the police service but does truly describe a lot of drivers you come across on the road. PQMS stands for Person of Questionable Mental Stability.

Speed Cameras

I have spoken at length to the first minister in charge of motoring law in the first Grump Republic and we are in agreement that speed cameras should stay. Considering they are reviled by many sections of the public, you might be thinking that this is a politically dangerous gambit. Motoring journalists and those on nine points particularly don't like them, but there's a certain sense of fair play about a speed camera.

For a start, they are mega conspicuous, to fit in with the brief that they are a speed deterrent at an accident blackspot; not a revenue stream. They are also logged on most SatNav systems (have I mentioned how good these are?). If that wasn't enough, they have a pre-camera warning sign at the side of the road. And if those reasons weren't enough, they have all the calibration marks on the road itself. So you know they're coming.

The ones they have in France have no warning signs, lurk at the side of the road in bushes where they can't be seen and are painted grey. They fire off at you like a sniper from a grassy knoll – sneak-cams.

One of the pleasures of a speed camera is seeing someone rip through them without realising they are there. It's the *schadenfreude* moment that we all enjoy and it's usually some boy racer who's got his mind elsewhere. When I see a speed camera go off I don't think, "Poor sod, another comrade crushed by the wheels of the state." I just think "heh, heh, heh". I'm not alone.

There is also a great pleasure to be had in timing your arrival at a speed camera to pass through at the maximum speed allowable without setting it off. The bloke-down-the-pub theory is that the tolerances are about 10 per cent, so for a 50 mph speed camera, that should only be activated at 56 mph. Given that my speedo lies to me by about 4 mph I should be able to have the needle on 59 mph without producing a tell-tale flash.

So far I've managed to go through with 55 mph registered on the dial with no consequence and I'm not sure how much braver I'm going to be. Were all the cars around me doing the same speed maybe I could be a little bolder, but they slow down to about 45 mph, which is plain chicken.

Speed Seminars

You can opt for one of these if you have no points on your licence and get done by a speed camera. Instead of getting three points, you go and sit in a room with a group of people who look like they've been beamed in from a Parish Council meeting – not the usual suspects.

Now I know what you're thinking and you're wrong. This wasn't a result of faulty Grump speed calibration. I thought I was in a 40 mph zone and it was a 30 mph zone. My crime against humanity was a paltry 36 mph – though it probably would have been about 44 mph had I not slammed the anchors on at the last moment when I saw the tell-tale yellow box and the heart-sinking Flash, Flash. (Though I imagine by the second flash the car must have been sideways.)

In these circumstances you get sent the option of having three points on your licence or you can pay to go to a Speed Seminar. Be assured, it's all fairly gentle stuff; there's no Alcoholics Anonymous-style admissions of guilt – "My name is Ivor Grump and I committed the offence of speeding."

They show you some videos and then you have to fill in one of the most hopelessly weighted questionnaires you could ever contemplate filling in. Seaside amusement arcade operators would blanch at the ridiculous bias that goes into analysing them.

It's a multiple-choice questionnaire about driving attitudes for which your answer will always be wrong. If you try and guess what the perceived "correct" answer should be, it will be wrong anyway – err on the side of caution and they deem you too slow and a hazard and a menace; err on the side of haste and it's wrong, wrong, wrong.

The whole point of it is to prove that you don't know as much as you think you do, but it's done with such sledgehammer subtlety that it defeats the object. I put mine in the bin on the way out. You are already aware you don't know everything, why did you set off the camera in the first place?

Average Speed Cameras

The reason that some motorists – like yours truly – are more accepting of isolated speed cameras is that they now appreciate it could be a lot worse. The average speed camera spoils everybody's fun. From the moment you pass into the realm of the average speed camera everything turns beige; it's a monotonous 50 mph and it feels like you're doing about 20 mph.

This could be a foretaste of things to come when speeds are regulated by GPS and excesses of the speed limit are transmitted to Big Brother (that's the Orwellian state apparatus, not Davina McCall).

Average speed cameras are a sinister first stage in a progression that will ultimately end with the thought police. They are also annoyingly effective, or thrillingly effective, depending on whether you're in a hurry or working on replacing the central-reservation barrier.

Clamps, Towing and Craning

Car clamps, car towing and car removing should all be consigned to the dustbin of history. They are a waste of resources and a source of unnecessary emissions – and that's not just from the drivers who get clamped.

Drivers have a points-based penalty system and cars should have the same thing too. Rack up 12 points in a three-year period and the car goes off to the crusher. Points would only be given for serious, clampable offences. Instead of getting a clamp that has to be put in place and then removed by a cave troll, a simple ticket backed up by four digital photos would suffice.

Now that the DVLA have a computerised system for dealing with MOTs, road tax and insurance, the administration of car-based points would be a computer project even this government couldn't mess up.

It would be a massive deterrent, because it could potentially affect the resale value of any car. What's more, it's a beautifully progressive tax. The higher the value of your car, the more you stand to lose by getting points on it. So the rich could no longer regard parking tickets as a form of parking charge, they would have to start thinking where they left their car.

Craning cars for parking offences is a waste of time because the crane lorries block off roads and inconvenience other motorists. Under the Grump system crane lorries would only pick up 12-pointers. They would be the equivalent of the Grim Reaper, administering that last fateful ride to the ceremonial crushing ground. To give them a sense of theatre, it might be fun to dress up one of the operators in the cowl or maybe issue them with black T-shirts emblazoned with a glinting scythe and play some appropriate music. Certainly not, "I Like Driving in my Car" by Madness.

The EU is not in favour of public executions, but this would be the closest we could get.

Parking Enforcement Officers

They used to be called traffic wardens but these days they're known as Parking Enforcement Officers. The essential requirement of the job is to have skin thicker than a rhino's hindquarters or not to understand much English, so that all the vitriol thrown at them goes right over their heads. Swear at them in Lithuanian, though, and you might get a result.

It would be easy to characterise PEOs as stupid, lazy, vindictive, hypocritical, fire-engine ticketing, inconsistent dolts. Actually, yes, that was very easy.

Everyone has their own special parking enforcement officer story but as the young Michael Jackson sang before his sad demise in 2009, "One bad apple don't spoil the whole bunch, girl." And for every one diamond-geezer parking enforcement officer who turns a blind eye to a pregnant woman leaving her car on a yellow line outside the pharmacy, there are 99 who would give her a ticket. And probably another three who would have her towed.

These days the paperwork has been cut down by issuing them with handy little digital cameras equipped with a suitable flash. The flash isn't needed for the photo, it's there so they know they're pointing the camera in the right direction. To comply with Health and Safety Standards, local councils have to ensure that their parking officers are kept nice and weatherproof at all times, so they are also issued with a small PVC tent through which someone has cut arm holes and legholes and applied haphazard amounts of reflective tape. In theory this is so that motorists can see them and take necessary action to avoid them if they step out into the road during the hours of darkness. In practice, it allows motorists to zero in on them like a guided missile.

NB: My mother met the most polite Parking Enforcement Officer in the world when she left her car on a single yellow line in Doncaster. She saw four of them walking along the pavement together in their peaked caps and uniforms and decided it was better to confess what she'd done before nipping into the newsagents. The young lad who she stopped smiled at her and said, "It's all right, love we're not traffic wardens, we're in a band."

Parking Appeals

Because there is so much pressure placed on parking enforcement officers to rack up their quota of tickets, hundreds and thousands are issued on a very thin pretext, or no text at all. They work on the inertia principal, that people won't be bothered to claim their legitimate right of appeal because it's too much trouble. Don't be put off. The parking appeals officer is a very nice man or woman, and upheld my complaint against the Nazis of Sutton who failed to accept that I had 37 minutes left on my parking ticket.... Even if he or she did describe one of my arguments as "fatuous".

Grump Enforcement Officer

Lead from the front, that's what I say. I would be prepared to become a parking enforcement officer in the Grump Republic under the following conditions.

Councils who stick single yellow lines on perfectly parkable roads so that they can force motorists into paying car parks will be named and shamed. Council leaders who are found to be operating this policy (and that would be virtually all of them) will have double yellow lines placed on the inner drives and parking spaces of their private houses and made to park in the nearest public car park. I would prioritise tickets for cars:

1) Whose value was over £25,000

2) Or just looked a bit flash

3) That had personalised number plates

4) That were gleamingly clean (if their owners have got enough time to clean their cars to perfection then they can find time to park them in the right place)

I would try and avoid giving tickets to cars:

A) That had child seats in them

B) That were over ten years old

C) Which looked like they belonged to an old person

D) That were dirty

I would be the Robin Hood of parking, except not the BBC's version of Robin Hood which is such a bunch of strung-out nonsense that it makes you yearn for the Kevin Costner film version with him as "Rab-inn of Lax-ley".

Congestion Charging

For those who want to take their car into central London and feel confident they have a bank loan big enough to afford the parking, then the congestion charge is a mere bagatelle. Pay it and be damned. The irony is that it hasn't improved the speed of the traffic through the centre of London, it's just given the mayor a bit of bubbly for the Christmas party. Gotta have a bit of bubbly for the Christmas party. Ken had a great idea for charging 4x4s an eye-watering level of cash for going into the zone and the prats at Porsche protested. It was a fabulous idea. One simply does not need a car capable of trekking up a grouse moor, or a 1 in 3 loose-shale incline, in the city.

Accident Voyeurs

Rubber neckers are the scum of the earth. There is nothing more pathetic than a group of ghoulish spectators that gather at the scene of an accident to poke their noses into someone else's misfortune. Almost as bad are the cars passing on the opposite side of the road or carriageway, which slow down to have an extended gawp as they go past. This has a knock-on effect and creates two traffic jams, one behind the accident and one on the opposite side of the road.

Sometimes one of the cretinous voyeurs driving in the opposite direction will take their eyes off the road in front of them for too long and have a separate accident. These are the kind of people you would dearly hope find their way into the Darwin awards – the posthumous awards for the most stupid ways to send yourself six feet under. It's the same quality of moron who is the last to hear the ambulance siren and the last to see the flashing blue light of the fire engine as it fills their rear-view mirror, like the alien spacecraft in *Close Encounters*.

Grump Tip: If you're at a set of traffic lights, waiting on red, and there is an enormous fire engine behind you with its lights flashing and its sirens wailing, it's okay to go through that light to let it past. Other people are aware of what they do, why it's there, and why it needs to get through quickly.

Perhaps in a parallel universe there isn't such a thing as a Grump Republic. Maybe there's a Voyeur's Paradise where the minutiae of everybody else's affairs can be studied in glorious detail, like *Big Brother* (that's the Davina McCall programme, not the Orwellian state apparatus). In Voyeur's Paradise there would be a neon display on all emergency vehicles telling you what drama was unfolding and where they were going, in case you wanted to drop by with your camera phone and get it all on YouTube.

On an ambulance you'd get a rolling screen with: ROAD TRAFFIC ACCIDENT, GRESWELL ST. SEVERAL DEAD.

On a police car you'd get a rolling screen with: DOMESTIC DISTURBANCE, ROMSEY ROAD, HUSBAND HAS KNIFE.

On a fire engine you'd get a rolling screen with: FIRE ALARM, ANOVA BOOKS, PROBABLY YET ANOTHER FALSE ALARM DUE TO FAULTY SENSOR.

Not Dogging, Actually

Clandestine Asian love affairs or romances can often be mistaken for something else. My friend Bhopindar fell in love with a girl who was a different caste to him and who he couldn't see openly anywhere near where they both lived for fear that her family would find out. So he would pick up his future wife and they would drive to car parks and have long intense conversations over cups of tea; there was a bit of hand holding and very little else.

One day someone must have reported a couple parked at a distance from other cars, in a notorious dogging car park. The local constabulary roared into the car park and ran over to his car expecting to catch them in flagrante. When they opened the door Bhopindar had his hands on her thermos and was discussing when his guru thought the omens might be right.

To their credit, the police were very apologetic, but Bhopindar told me the most embarrassing thing about the whole incident was not knowing what dogging was and having to ask several questions to be certain.

THE JOY OF
MOTORWAYS

Brown Signs

Brown is the colour of local interest, right the way across Europe. Fahren, fahren, fahren, auf dem autobahn, as Kraftwerk liked to do; allez sur l'autoroute, or travel by motorway and you'll be assailed by large brown signs wherever you go, promoting places of interest a few miles off the motorway that you can visit if you've got the time. It could be a local abbey, a castle, a countryside park or even a stately home. There might be a famous race track or a historic battle site waiting to be discovered ten minutes from the next junction.

So tell me. How does that explain Alton Towers being signposted off the M6? You could fit whole countries between the M6 turn-off for Alton Towers and Alton Towers itself. It's miles away. Try telling that to the kids when you've just announced, "It shouldn't be long, look, there's the sign now..."

But at least anything that gets its own brown sign in the UK is worth a visit. In France they have brown signs erected for a hole in the ground surrounded by three stones. Visitez Les Trois Pierres Miraculous. There are so few places of interest that they have to resort to universal illustrations of women in traditional dress clutching ducks, goats and cheese.

It's the French nation's bad luck that Le Corbusier was one of theirs. Travel south from Calais towards the Alps or the Mediterranean and what they ought to put on the brown signs is "Ici Le Crap Architecture". To the south the road becomes known as the Route du Soleil. Well up north it's the Route du Crap Tower Block. Kilometre after kilometre looks like Marineville at the start of *Stingray* – except they don't disappear conveniently underground. Cumbernauld in Scotland looks like Bath compared to some of the monstrosities you can view from the autoroutes of France.

Waiting for Godot

Off the top of my head, I can't remember the former profession of the tramp in *Waiting for Godot*. The irony of Godot in Samuel Beckett's play – and I don't think I'm giving away too many surprises here – is that Godot never turns up. The other tramps spend their hours killing time and waiting for Godot, hence the phrase, "It's like waiting for…"

So my guess is that he used to be a roads engineer. Godot's modern-day equivalent is struck with the same malaise of never getting round to doing anything. He is plagued by the questions that revolve around his head about the futility of life and our sad short time on this small spinning globe. Why are we here? Isn't there something better we could be doing? And if I improve this road surely that means that people get to where they're going and don't have time to think about the bigger picture; the meaning of life.

On the motorways this takes the form of coning off lanes, creating massive contra-flows controlled by average speed cameras, but never actually doing any road engineering. There's just so much of it to do, where do you start? What's the point...oh, let's do another survey and delay the moment we have to get started.

Roadworks: It's My Builder's Fault

The other theory I have to explain our miles of coned-off lanes, where there is little apparent roadwork going on, is that the Highways Agency has employed my builder to do it all. My builder has an amazing ability to sequence delays and shortfalls to guarantee continuous non-activity on a project. "The bricks haven't turned up, I'm waiting for the right bricks," is one of his favourites. Then, when the bricks arrive, "The bricklayer's on another job now." When bricks and bricklayer are in harmony the mini-digger needed to dig out the footings breaks down and they have to send away to Ulan Bator for a spare part. During which time, they take the bricks away for another job and we're back to excuse No.1 again.

I'm sure if Tony was in charge of the road repair programme he could introduce new and wonderful reasons to delay projects. "We left the tarmac-laying machine in the yard and someone stole it," or "was it the A329 you wanted resurfacing, we've just done the A392" and "we didn't have enough barrier for the whole bypass, so we had to leave gaps every 20 metres. That is what you wanted...?"

The fact that ruins this theory is that sometimes, somewhere in the UK, road projects do get finished. And that's not his style at all.

People Who Watch Motorway Traffic

Why? You see people watching the traffic from motorway bridges and it's hard to fathom...unless they're in uniform and holding a speed gun. What is the allure of the three-lane carriageway rushing relentlessly past? In my youth, I concede, out of boredom you might consider going down to look at the motorway if nobody had a football and you'd tried the patience of everyone in your street with Knockdown Ginger. But these days there is multi-channel television, the Internet, Xbox360 and PlayStations. How can motorway voyeurism compete when you can't do it from your sofa and it gives you lead poisoning?

Mile for mile travelled, motorways are the safest roads to drive on. So for the ghoulish who trek down there hoping to see vehicles overturned like it was the latest Stallone movie, it's a wasted trip. Accidents are a rarity. If your day is so dull that you have to go out and look for accidents then I recommend you try your nearest skateboarding park. There you will be assured of a proportionately high number of accidents for every centimetre travelled.

Motorway Services – Bungs and Buddhism

You were probably waiting to see how long it would take to get to this one, but compared to many nations' motorway services, ours are no different. The only major disparity between service areas here and on the continent is that ours are full of football club managers getting bungs in brown paper bags. If you could clear out all the drug deals, pay-offs, bungs and nefarious meetings that go on in motorway service areas there'd be tumbleweed blowing through.

It's become a passing hobby of mine that when I have to use a motorway service area, I try and spot the most obvious dodgy deal. The giveaway is two blokes sitting in the front seats of their car talking to each other and then breaking off when you pass by.

Motorway services also bring out the Buddhist in me. The Buddhist philosophy and its take on the human condition is one that occupies a great deal of internalised Grump debate.

The question is this: Have we fallen from the created status as a result of original sin? Or are we, rather, a product of the periodical manifestation of the ultimate reality, and thus ignoring our true spiritual destiny? Do we have an innate soul that predated our birth? Is our personal character temporary, or do we keep it for a further existence? Is our ultimate destination limited to this present existence, or do we inherit an eternal one, and if eternal, is it personal or impersonal? Most importantly - is the service area on the opposite carriage-way better than ours? It always bloody looks like it is.

You stop one side of the motorway and the opposite side is always less busy, it's bound to be cleaner and have more outlets open and have a greater range of food. Trust your luck, there's no footbridge on this one either. Buddhism teaches that it is the human condition to always want more – more personal possessions, more happiness, more security. The lesson motorway service areas teach us is that we may want these things, but we cannot have them.

Motorway Catering

Motorway catering can bring you the highs and the lows of eating out. The highs being the bill; the lows being the temperature, the quality, the quantity, the service, and the standards of hygiene.

Often when inspecting cafeteria-style restaurants, local authorities dispense with a food standards officer and bring in an archaeologist to date some of the Danish pastries. It's not uncommon to find a selection of pastries that can be dated back to the stone age and restaurant users often choose to exhibit them or donate them to a local museum rather than place their teeth anywhere near them.

The reason that companies can get away with serving such unmentionable toot is that, well, where else are you going to go? The fact that they have introduced Burger King franchises into many service areas hasn't helped. They're either closed or have one cheeseburger and some dessicated fries left. Or they have a queue of 60 schoolchildren who've just got off a coach.

Opt for the Little Chef in the corner of the car park and as you walk in you're met by the eyes of 60 hungry people all wondering where their food has got to while the one chef who's bothered to turn up for work swears it would be easier working in Hell's Kitchen the night after Gordon's had another exposé in the *News of the World*.

I quite like the concept that another top TV chef, Heston Blumenthal, got his name thanks to his parents' love of Heston services on the M4. That might be one of the explanations for Heston's trial partnership with Little Chef a few years back – cooking on the move is in his blood. As I remember, the champion of molecular gastronomy was all for changing the menu to include some very un-Little-Chef-like dishes such as snail porridge, mustard ice cream and creosote pudding with a Ronseal glaze. Yummy.

Leaving the Service Area

Having stopped at a motorway service area, I'm a big fan of getting back on the same motorway and going in the same direction I was going before. That's why I don't much like the service stations that serve both carriageways. You're directed over bridges or under roads via a Milton Keynesian series of roundabouts and it's impossible to remember which way you've come, because you never rejoin the motorway the way you came off it. At the back of your mind there is a nagging fear that you're going to rejoin heading north when you wanted to be heading south – and then there's no turn-off for 24 miles. I know someone who stopped at one of the service areas near the Severn Bridge, got back on the motorway to cross into Wales and before she knew it she was heading back to Bristol. To make matters worse she decided to head south on the M5 to turn round, got stuck in traffic, was upset at being very late, found what she thought was the correct exit to head back towards Wales, realised at the last minute she was heading back down the M4 towards London but couldn't change lanes quick enough. In all, it took her three hours to get back to the Severn Bridge, by which time she was bursting to go to the toilet and had to stop at the same services again.

I'm convinced that all these examples of bewildered pensioners driving on the wrong side of the motorway start off at the exits of motorway services. Even when there's only one exit.

Hello Moto

Aiming to shed their tired image, the old Granada motorway services decided to adopt a sophisticated continental sheen by rebranding themselves as Moto. Motorists visiting Moto will notice a range of unique Moto signs the minute they enter the service area.

The Highway Code tells us that signs with blue circles give us a positive instruction. So at Southwaite service station on the M6 there's a sign of a picnic table inside a blue circle – this sign is essentially telling us – "you must picnic". Not only that, the thoughtful people at Moto have provided a children's play area and to indicate it there is a sign of a child's rocking horse inside a blue circle – "you must rocking horse". Of slightly more dubious nature is the one they've designed for the dog fouling area. It's a sign of a Scotty dog inside a blue circle, essentially meaning – "you must dog". Now that's what I call rebranding.

The Tamworth M42 Services

On the same lines, the Highway Code also tells us that signs within red circles are mostly prohibitive – meaning whatever activity is going on in the red circle, well that's just not allowed.

If you were to visit Tamworth services on the M42, strictly adhering to the Highway Code wouldn't get you out of the car park. There's a pedestrian crossing that's guarded by a sign that means "no pedestrians". There's a "two-way traffic ahead" sign in a red circle – meaning "no two-way traffic ahead". But the highlight is a "give way" sign in a red circle – meaning "don't give way".

In the UK we have learned to ignore things like this. If it were Japan, there would be a queue of cars waiting obediently by the sign until it was changed. There seriously would. I was once shouted at by an elderly Japanese man in the middle of Tokyo at 3 a.m. There was no traffic about at all – only me and him on an empty back street. He stopped because the pedestrian crossing light had turned to red. When I ignored the sign he got very angry. He couldn't chase me, though, because he had to wait for the light.

Tailbacks

A great many things associated with motorways make me grumpy. As I think I might have touched on. But nothing in God's firmament makes me more grumpy than a motorway queue travelling at a differential speed. I can cope with the wait, I can cope with the plans-for-the-day-thrown-out-of-the-window. I cannot cope with the fact that THEIR LANE is going faster than MY LANE. If the misery is spread out evenly and we are all stopped or we all edge forward at the same hopeless rate of progress that is fine, I can accept it.

What makes me angry is that by the law of averages sooner or later I ought to end up in the lane that goes faster than the other two lanes. It never happens. I always pick the lane that goes the slowest. To increase my chances of going in the second fastest lane or even the dizzy heights of the fastest lane (fastest being a relative term) I vary it. Sometimes I'll pick the slow lane, sometimes the middle and often the outside lane. It's always the wrong lane.

What makes the experience doubly worse is that the minute my lane starts to show any sign of winning the contest OTHER BASTARDS TRY AND GET IN IT. You can see them looking in their rear-view mirrors as you edge ahead and even before they indicate their intentions they're angling their vehicle across to force you to let them in. I don't, I keep my course straight and true and it's up to them to see how much their no-claims bonus is worth. They either give up or their lane gets a sudden spurt forward and they successfully bully the car in front of mine to let them in.

My greatest pleasure then is to see my lane slow down and the lane they've just left speed up. It's the only slight glimmer of entertainment you can have in a traffic queue, to see impatient cars making a series of dodgy moves that get them nowhere.

GRUMPIA LAW decrees that once you slow to less than 10 mph in a traffic tailback on a motorway or dual carriageway – from that point on you must stay in the lane you have chosen. This is your Lane of Destiny. Should you try and move out of your Lane of Destiny for any other reason than the car in front has stopped, then your car will receive three crusher points.

Three Lanes Into Two

Another grumpfest of mine is the people who cruise up the outside when three lanes merge into two as they approach roadworks.

Being Brits we're very good about getting into queues and most of us get in a stationary line early, leaving the outside lane free for BMWs to cruise down and push in at the end by the cones. Who does it? Volvo drivers? Occasionally. Honda Civic drivers? Never. BMW drivers? All the time. It's the Germanic nature of the cars they're driving that forces them to do it. Either that or they're just complete turds.

And in a way it's our own fault; if we got into the habit of using all three lanes when there were roadworks then there wouldn't be that oh-so inviting yawning chasm for them to drive down. In urban areas they actually tell you to use all three lanes – or all two lanes before it narrows to one – because otherwise the queue tails back too far.

So if you're one of those queue jumpers you could actually justify your selfish actions by pointing to the inside queue-sitters as self-righteous tarmac-huggers.

To counteract the queue jumpers, motorists, van and lorry drivers occasionally place their car half in the middle lane and half in the outside lane to prevent anyone from getting past. They are heroes. My own technique is to block off the whole lane and creep along only as fast as the car that was previously in front of me, thus maintaining the fairness and integrity of the queue. Drivers behind can get very agitated about this, but it's better that they should be put out than everybody else.

Gridlocks

Every once in a while a slow-moving tailback turns into a completely stopped snarl-up. Carriageways grind to a halt and people get out of their cars to see what's going on.

It feels strangely anarchic to be walking along in the outside lane of a motorway, even if you are part of a body of people all doing the same thing. As a youth, I pushed a car along in the outside lane of the M5 near Bridgewater in the middle of a very slow-moving August traffic jam and it was thrilling. For about twenty years afterwards I would regale people in the car whenever we passed the very spot. "I pushed a car along there once" became one of my top anecdotes. Right up there with my story about how I jammed the hop-picking machinery.

But I digress. When you're all stuck together on the motorway there's a palpable sense of community spirit. News about what might be the cause of the hold-up is readily passed on. People talk and chat, it's so much more sociable than a slow, grim crawl where everyone is bad tempered and out for themselves. In those circumstances the police should authorise one of those layby-dwelling tea 'n' coffee 'n' snacks caravans to hotfoot it up the hard shoulder and open for business. They'd offer a stress-relief service to agitated motorists and do some great trade into the bargain. You could probably deploy one full-time going north on the elevated section of the M6 through Birmingham, or going south on the M6 as you approach Birmingham.

Motorway Warning Signs

Police get very frustrated when people don't slow down for the variable speed warning signs that appear on motorways. They're the ones that announce that the speed limit has suddenly changed to 60 mph or 50 mph or 40 mph.

My view is that they're not really speed limits at all, but a kindly warning: "Be prepared to slow down to... 60 mph if you see a lot of brake lights round the next corner."

The reason everyone except my mother-in-law ignores them is because 90 per cent of the time they're wrong. They're warning about an accident that took place several hours ago and the stoppage has long since been cleared, yet no one could be arsed to go along and change the signs back. Are all motorway patrolmen teenagers? "Durrr, I'll do it later, I promise." It undermines confidence in the whole system.

The only ones that are ever useful are the ones that say FOG. While you can see them you know there's no fog, but the minute they disappear...

Keeping Two Chevrons Apart

We all know it was John Major who was responsible for the Cones Hotline (and incidentally, am I the only person in this politically moribund world that thinks it was a landmark piece of government thinking?), but who invented keeping two chevrons apart?

There you are, cruising up the M6 north of Sandbach and out come the signs: "keep two chevrons apart". You look on the road and there they are, half a Citroën badge lovingly moulded into the tarmac every 20 yards (or 18.76 metres for those who'd sooner have an EU sticker on the back of their voiture). The grand plan is that you leave enough distance between the car in front's rear bumper and your own front bumper to see these two chevrons, thus guaranteeing that should the car in front slam on the anchors that you have enough stopping distance. That's the theory, anyway.

In practice, as soon as you leave two chevrons' distance between yourself and the car in front it's filled with two white vans and a Mondeo towing a glider. And that's at 70 mph or above.

When speeds drop to less than 50 mph you have to apply Grump's Theory of Car Spacing, which states that: If you think the distance between you and the car in front is too small to safely fit another car, another car will pull into it. Slow down to 50 mph and you will get the entire fleet of Norbert Dentressangle trying to fit itself between you and the car in front.

Tiredness Kills – Take a Break

One of Mrs Grump's favourite signs on motorways, and one which we heartily rubbish whenever we pass it, is the "Tiredness Kills" sign, which advertises a particular brand of women's magazine, namely *Take a Break*.

Why not Tiredness Kills – *Woman's Weekly*, Tiredness Kills – *Bella*, or even Tiredness Kills – *Hello!* At least the contradictory emotions of the last sign will have people sitting up and taking notice and not slumping back in their seats snoring for Britain.

Tiredness Kills – *Take a Break* is not even correct. It's pitiful, hard-to-believe stories about "the child I never knew" that kill the circulation of *Take a Break*, not bleary-eyed motorists struggling across the Somerset/Devon border.

My advice to the Ministry of Road Misery is to get some revenue from the buggers. How about: Tiredness Kills – Take a Break, Take a Kit-Kat. Now that could actually make some money which could be ploughed back into road improvements. Or get a wide variety of magazines to sponsor the signs: Tiredness Kills – *Total Trout*, Tiredness Kills – *Railway Modeller* or even Tiredness Kills – *Farmer's Weekly*.

The alternative to these lame signs is sheer Grump genius. Forget the visual impact of a sign, if you're half asleep at the wheel you won't notice them anyway. What you need is a great big blaring foghorn that sounds whenever you drive past it. That will certainly jolt you awake. They could be placed at random on particularly boring stretches of the motorway network (i.e. the entire length of the M1 south of Birmingham) just to keep drivers guessing.

BAD DRIVING HABITS

Overtaking When There's No Reason

Let's try a small exercise. Count with me: 1,001, 1,002, 1,003, 1,004, 1,005. That's the small amount of time that drivers will save by attempting the most perilous of overtaking moves. Some people – for the purpose of this exercise let's call them knobs – are prepared to swing out into the oncoming lane of a single carriageway road putting their passengers in danger, the car they're overtaking in danger, and any oncoming vehicle in danger. And all for what? To be five seconds further down the road. Late at night and early in the morning, when there are few cars about on the road, you might get an advantage from a nifty little overtaking move. To which I would say, "Good on you, mate." But on a Sunday afternoon, when you can see there's another seven or eight cars ahead, what is the cockamamie idea?

Don't get me wrong, I love to see well-handled cars travelling at speed, driven with skill and courtesy. Sometimes breathtakingly audacious moves on the road will have me chuckling – and the wife will back me up on this. Sometimes, the sensible option is to overtake the other side of the pedestrian island. If you can show a bit of vision, good luck to you.

But men who overtake for no reason clearly have small penises. It would be far better for us all if they took notice of their e.mail junk box and went away to get an extra 3" – a doubling of size has surely got to be worth it. They tend to drive cars like the Chrysler Crossfire or Toyota Celicas; cars with pretensions of sportiness that don't quite cut it. On a busy A-road you can see that there's a stack of traffic stuck behind a car pulling a boat up ahead and you know there's only eight miles to the next town when some of them will probably turn off, so you calculate:

X) Even if I overtook all of them I'd probably take six miles to do it in. So I'd go at my own faster speed for two miles.

Y) That's providing that no other vehicle pulls out onto the A-road in front of the car with the boat.

Z) And there might not be enough places to overtake in the next eight miles.

Making X + Y = ...
You're a twonk for even bothering to do the calculation. You take one look at the traffic and you think, sod it, that's what you do. Meanwhile, the boy racers will come piling past the first three cars in the little train, slotting in to gaps that were hardly there, making people brake hard and then realising that's as far as they're going to get.

Overtaking to Sneer

Comedian Michael McIntyre reckons that people always look across at the driver of the car they've just overtaken to have a good old sneer. "I've just overtaken you! Eat my exhaust!" It's very funny, but it's not completely true. For a start, you can only afford to do that on a motorway or one of those long straight French roads that stretch out into infinity. And unless you're driving a Citroën C2 or a Fiat 500, overtaking on a motorway isn't the most complex of manoeuvres – it's not like doing a stunt handbrake turn into a parking spot or a controlled four-wheel drift, tyres-a-smokin'.

I look across for all sorts of reasons:

a) To see if it was a woman or a man, from the silhouette you couldn't be sure.

b) To see if they really are on the phone, because they're driving like they are.

c) To see if he/she fits the stereotypical driver of that car – for instance Toyota MX5; unmarried woman in her twenties or a hairdresser.

d) To see if they are attractive (usually women).

e) If it's an unusual car, to see what kind of person's driving it.

f) If it's a version of my wife's car, to collect statistics on the kind of person driving it and to reassure her it's not more 50-year-old lesbian librarians.

g) From the height profile, to see if it's an old person or a midget. Or if a small child has taken it.

Overtaking When You're Slow

In my youth I used to drive a Citroën with a 600cc engine and overtaking anything in it was an intellectual exercise. All factors had to be taken into account. Was the topography going to be right (i.e. downhill or flat, never uphill)? The wind factor had to be calculated (a quick check of the rippling vinyl roof was enough to do that). What kind of road space lay ahead (was it going to be long enough)? If you were going to put yourself into the danger zone of an oncoming carriageway you needed something like the Bonneville Flats in front of you.

When all the omens were right, you needed a space to build up the tow from the car in front and then launch yourself out at the perfect moment, like a Tour de France sprinter going for the line in the last 150 metres. At that point you floored it.

There are few cars where you spend most of your time with the accelerator fully depressed – dodgems at fairs, maybe, or cheap go-karts – but this was a regular occurrence with the Citroën. The increase in speed was marginal, but marginal got you past.

The car creaked and groaned up to 60 mph or 65 mph downhill, then inched ahead of the car that was being overtaken and in an exultant moment you were past it and could pull in, you had overtaken and you had lived to tell the tale. Hallelujah!

When you're in a slow car on the motorway and you need to make a move into the outside lane, you get this all-consuming feeling of guilt that you shouldn't be there. You stick out like a sore thumb; like a tramp on a golf course, or a Premiership footballer in a library. The second a gap appears on your left and you've overtaken the crane or the road roller you want to get back to your comfort zone in the slow lane.

Middle-Lane Hoggers

In the pantheon of crap drivers – Middle-Lane Hoggers are right up there. Whereas people who cruise up the outside lane and try to push into queues know that they're being a little bit cheeky, middle-lane hoggers think they're brilliant drivers. These are the people who, given an empty three-lane carriageway, choose to drive in the middle lane.

What these smug, self-satisfied eejits don't realise is that they're committing an offence. The outside two lanes are overtaking lanes and if you're overtaking nothing, you shouldn't be there.

They think that as long as they're doing the statutory speed limit they have a divine right to whichever lane they choose because "nobody should be going faster than me, anyway". At which point they switch off from looking in the rear-view mirror, turn up their *Teach Yourself Spanish in the Car* CD and cruise.

After taking a precautionary look behind me for patrol cars, I like to nudge past them on the inside. This has the habit of waking them up. Or you can sit directly behind them and after a couple of miles they'll suddenly realise there are other vehicles on the motorway apart from them and grudgingly indicate to move over. Middle-lane hoggers must drive truckers spare. The trait isn't gender specific or car marque specific or age specific, but mostly it's coffin-dodgers in VWs.

The Saddest Hogger of Them All

The saddest middle-lane hogger of them all is the one that speeds up the minute you go to overtake them in the outside lane. I thought this was a pathetic beta or gamma male characteristic, but I've noticed women doing it too. They're trundling along at 70 mph and as you approach them you realise that they're not going to pull into the empty inside lane – so you speed up to 75 mph and make a move for the outside lane. They spot you and speed up to 75 mph too. You realise 75 mph isn't going to be enough and you're committed to the outside lane now, so you speed up to 80 mph. They do too. So you think, sod it, I'm not going to back down now and speed up to 85 mph. All of a sudden this piece of human excrement with a driving licence has accelerated from 70 mph to 80 mph+ in a bid to keep in front of a car that is going to overtake him anyway. Madness.

I've witnessed the same characteristic in pond fish. They rush to compete for food thrown into a pond, whether they need it or not – they can't stop themselves. The brain equivalency of the hogger is similar.

Outside-Lane Hoggers

More dangerous, but more observant than the middle-lane hogger is the outside-lane hogger. To hog in the outside lane requires a car that will cruise at 85 mph and the unshifting belief that whatever speed they choose to do above the old speed limit… is the new speed limit. Thus, this gives them the authority to sit in the outside lane and cruise there impervious to any other outside-lane hoggers who believe the new speed limit should be at least ten miles an hour quicker, so get the hell out of the way! You never see outside lane hoggers doing under 70 mph. That's because under 70 mph they know they shouldn't be there. At 71 mph they know that neither of you is in the right and possession of the lane is nine tenths of the law and actually, drivers are not supposed to communicate with flashed headlights and that isn't the correct hand gesture for "I am going straight on".

Flashers

Flashers may be in a hell of a hurry to get somewhere but they're incredibly slow on the uptake. Flashing at someone is both an art and a science and one in which it helps to know about the law of diminishing returns. Come up behind someone at speed, flash your lights, and they might move over. Flash your lights twice and they might hesitate a bit before moving over. Flash three times and that person will definitely not move over, unless you turn into an emergency services vehicle.

Me? I slow down if I'm flashed. If someone comes up behind me at speed, just as I'm about to overtake a lorry, and flashes that I should have let them go through first, my revs suffer badly. I cut my speed back to barely more than the vehicle I was about to pass with gusto and crawl past like a truck on the limiter. Should the impatient vehicle behind not react well to this manoeuvre and flash again, then I give a little wave, the kind a cheery pensioner would do. Then I slow down, indicate left and let the vehicle I was going to overtake pass me, and pull in behind it, allowing my new friend to go through first – which is what he wanted.

On good days, this whole process can take several minutes. Hopefully the thought will strike the flasher at some stage that if he hadn't been such a knob, he would have got past a lot quicker.

Instead of designing cars that have endless unnecessary detail, what motor manufacturers really should invest in is a friendly Ooops-you-probably-haven't-realised-you're-in-the-wrong-lane headlight flash. A courtesy flash that is a kind of friendly alert, not a Get-the-hell-out-of-my-way.

Bumper Huggers

Flashers and Bumper Huggers are closely related sub-species. They both want you to hurry up and get out of their way. The flashing bumper hugger is the most aggressive of the species, but if he gets too close to your rear bumper then you can't see the full Xenon glory of his intolerant flash.

Unflashing Bumper Huggers are the ones who have worked out that flashing the driver in front is a self-defeating action. Instead, they choose to pressurize you by looming large in the rear-view mirror.

Someone I know, who is similarly disposed towards bumper huggers, had this unnerving habit of turning his lights on suddenly, thus giving the impression that he was braking. When you have a car right on your tail, the sudden application of brakes from the car in front gives someone very little time to react.

I would never contemplate it, because it's so utterly dangerous. What I do is slow down. On *Top Gear* James May is known as Captain Slow for his inability to keep up. I like to think I become Field Marshal Slow when faced with a bumper hugger.

Hard-Shoulder Cruisers

These are the modern-day equivalent of Mr Toad from *Toad of Toad Hall*. Casually pushing into the front of a queue when everybody's queued nicely may be the action of a bicycle-seat sniffer, but it's not illegal. Deciding that you can't be fagged to queue when there's a tailback on the motorway and using the hard shoulder as your personal escape lane is illegal, dangerous, and one of the best ways to pick up a puncture. That would be an easy six Crusher Points under the new regime, with exceptions for pregnant women en route to hospital and anyone on their way to assassinate Michael Winner.

Inbetweeners and Cat's-Eye Cleaners

Not necessarily a candidate for the Grump Gulags, but certainly this transgressor could use time in some kind of motoring correctional facility. The middle-lane hogger and the outside-lane hogger might not have much going for them but at least they know which lane they're in – even if they shouldn't be in it. The inbetweener isn't sure. Typically he is mostly in the outside lane, but his nearside tyre is straying over the white line so that he is 85 per cent in the outside lane and 15 per cent in the middle lane. Basically, he is an indecisive outside-lane hogger, but with none of the speed or assurance and a morbid fear of barriers. Either that or he has his eyes shut and is steering by means of the thumpa-thumpa-thumpa-thumpa sound of his wheels running over the cats' eyes.

Leaving-It-Late Lane Choppers

I have a sneaking admiration for the skilled lane choppers who can exercise the last-minute chop without causing anyone to brake or swear. I have a contempt for the inexpert lane chopper and wish him nothing but an unhappy life. The leaving-it-late lane choppers are the cars who zoom up behind you on a dual carriageway or motorway as you are approaching an exit. Instead of pulling into the inside lane in front of you, they keep on going into the exit road in one smooth perfect motion.

If people can do that in front of me without causing me to brake, then good luck to them, they are blessed with good timing and I cheer them on their way. The problem is, not many people are. Instead of pulling across in one swift movement, they squeeze between you and the car in front, then jab their brakes on hard as though they were making an emergency stop, then shoot off left.

Getting into the right lane early would have cost them maybe five or six seconds, but no, their time is more important than my brake pads. Sometimes they do it when there isn't even a gap. They pull alongside you in the centre lane with their indicator indicating left, as though they have some divine right to be let in, and command that you allow a gap. This often happens at the junction where I leave the dual carriageway and it is my delight to keep an eye out for the late lane chopper in my driver wing mirror. As he pulls alongside and frantically signals to be let in to my lane, I pretend that I am not only going straight on and adjust the stereo as though I haven't seen him. Right at the last minute, when all hope is lost and he is committed to going straight on, I indicate left and nip off down the exit, leaving him to rue his encounter with a fully fledged grump behind the wheel of the Grumpmobile.

NO DIRECTIONS HOME

SatNav Victims

SatNavs are a wonderful invention. There are many towering figures in automotive history: Gottlieb Daimler, Karl Benz, Otto Diesel, Felix Wankel, to which should be added the name Jurgen SatNav.

How many relationships has this device saved? Luckily, I am blessed with that most extraordinary of female creatures, a wife who is a brilliant map reader. And though we've had our moments in far-flung cul-de-sacs that "should have been Junction 14 on the M11" and taken interesting diversions into industrial estates, "I never knew that's where they made Ginsters pies," I count myself as blessed.

There are many husbands and wives out there who couldn't find their own house in a road atlas, let alone plan a route to a holiday destination or a distant wedding. For these people, the SatNav has been a marriage saver.

Not only does it cut out all the stress of decision making by telling you which route to take, it also tells you the distance you have to travel and exactly how late you're going to be when you get there.

So what makes me really angry is when you see that cringing band of protozoa known as SatNav Victims.

SatNav Victims are the people who turn up in a *Daily Mail* comedy photo news item having stuffed their car into a footpath entrance, "because the SatNav told them to". To a man they are all spineless, chinless wonders who trip over paving slabs and sue councils, who think it's the world's job to wipe their arse.

"My SatNav tried to drive me over a cliff!" screams the headline – well, good, it's just a pity that you didn't manage to carry out the instruction. In fact, that's one example of an electronic aid showing intelligent judgement; clearly realising that their owners were too dumb to live and giving them a fate that Darwin would have approved of.

Honestly, I ask you. You're driving along a road and there's a flat, bluey green thing on the horizon with little white dots that look like sails. It's the sea. Try not to drive into it.

SatNav Rage

The only time that SatNavs are a pain in the proverbial is when their city centre maps haven't been updated and they ask you to turn the wrong way into a one-way street. It's at those times that the calm and patient voice of

"Jane" (who you've selected for her unflustered instructions and close resemblance to Radio 4's Charlotte Green) starts to sound a bit judgemental. She's saying "make a U-turn", but you know deep down she's thinking "make a U-turn, tosser".

SatNav Fun

Incidentally, a great practical joke to play on a friend who is about to take a motoring holiday to the continent armed with their SatNav is to secretly swap the memory card on his TomTom Go. Instead of heading abroad with comprehensive details of roads from Andorra to Zermatt, substitute the 56k map of Legoland in Holland (available as a free download). Imagine the hoots of amusement when he gets to Calais, switches it on and finds all roads lead to just outside Amsterdam.

However, you don't need the wrong set of maps to waste a day in Europe. I love the story about the coach driver who took some booze-cruisers on a Channel-hopping trip to Lille in France. Sadly, for the happy shoppers, he dialled Lille in Belgium into his SatNav, which is the other side of Antwerp. They managed 45 minutes shopping in a small Belgian village before heading back to the ferry.

Another great joke – and one for all the family – is to remove all the standard voices on the SatNav. In their place, insert one from the rude section of a SatNav voices website. You can choose from Tina Tourettes, Bad Santa, Sex Toy Susan, Tony Tourettes, Randy Rob and Naughtie Natalie. The fun starts from the very first expletive-drenched road direction and lasts for ages…till maybe the fourth road direction.

Road Maps

The SatNav has given us all a joyous release from that instrument of torture – the road map. The fold-out variety has all the user-friendliness of a broadsheet newspaper on a packed tube train. Yes, they're perfectly fine laid out on a dining-room table where they give an impressive sense of scale and distance. The big snag comes when you want to read them in the car, which, as the phrase "road map" gives away, is the place where you probably will want to read them most.

Once unfolded in a car they cease to be an inanimate object; they become like a mogwai you've fed after midnight; they become a gremlin. They develop a personality of their own and are intent on presenting the wrong side whenever they can.

They will crease along unexpected lines, slap into the driver's face at the slightest zephyr, do their best to hide the gearstick and tuck themselves neatly under the handbrake. And they're impossible to read. If you try and give them a bit of summary discipline they tear. After you have lost your patience and thrown in the towel, they are about as easy to fold up as it would be to wallpaper the inside of your car.

London A-Z

In some far-flung Asian country there's a man who spent 12 years inscribing the whole of the Koran onto the back of a postage stamp. After another six years spent inscribing the bible onto a pinhead, he obviously moved to London and helped the publishers of the London A-Z cram an unreasonable amount of roads onto a single page.

The London A-Z is the only popular book that gives people with 20/20 vision feelings of inadequacy. It has road names jammed into nano-spaces and the type set at 5-point. The ingredients list of chocolate bars looks like an advertising hoarding compared to the A-Z lettering.

Reading it is a depressing experience. You go to the index and discover the grid square where your chosen road is located. You trot along to the grid square and it looks like a child has been let loose with an etch-a-sketch over the top of a low-scoring scrabble game. The road names are split into unreadable chunks as the line of the road twists and turns and branches and spurs– WORT-HING-TON RO-AD.

Finding an undivided four-syllable word in one piece is like finding Wally in *Where's Wally?* Or WAL-LY as the A-Z would have it.

But, not content with peddling us the conventional size A-Z, if you value maximum pocket space above blindness there's a mini edition too. A mini-edition! In fact, there's a growing suspicion that SpecSavers sponsored the mini edition, which can only be properly read by small babies whose corneas are yet to harden.

Road Atlases

These are far more practical than a road map, but still in the stone age compared to a digital navigation device. Often they come with a helpful ring binder to allow the pages to open flat on your lap. The gentlest of tugs will thus remove a page as though it were perforated along the edge – the bigger the page, the swifter the exit. In fact most perforated sheets have a higher resistance to removal than a ring-bound road atlas.

Road atlases have been designed by sadists who have successfully divided the map pages so that major conurbations of the UK all fall on the corners of pages. Their trickiest task is to try and get Manchester and Liverpool both on corners. Similarly, the coordinates of the nation's major road intersections, pinch points and traffic blackspots are all fed into a computer to make sure they too can be located on the very bottom of Page 52 only to re-appear in a strangely unrecognizable form on Page 66.

Grump's Law of Road Atlases

The first page to fall out will be the one you really need. Interestingly (or not, and probably not), there is a good scientific reason for this, as the page you are likely to use the most will get the most thumb-age and so is likely to be the first to fall like a gentle autumn leaf.

Asking Directions from a Local

We're always being told by fat-tongued cockney chefs that getting things locally is good. If not lovely. This doesn't apply to directions. Get your directions locally and you're likely to end up miles from where you want to go. Most people haven't a clue about the names of the roads nearby unless:

a) It's the road they live in
b) They're close to a road sign they can read
c) It's the High Street

And if they do profess to know the route they'll end up sending you all the way round the houses to get there. Non-motorists will send you via the footpaths. My advice for anyone thinking about asking a local for directions is: just get a vague idea of the direction you need to go in, and the distance and quit while you're ahead.

It's not wilful deception, these people sincerely want to help. It's just that *Britain's Got Talent* moment when the spotlight is upon them and they blurt stuff out.

There are many things that locals don't know the names of but especially churches. Our godless society has produced a population that has no idea what the churches are called any more – or what they're there for.

Remembering Road Directions

If you've ignored the advice of never ask a local, then don't compound your folly by asking an old local, or worse still, an old local couple. By the time you've actually got your directions, the event you were travelling to will have finished. Ask an old local and not only will you get directions, you'll get stories and histories and little anecdotes about the places you will pass en route, plus chuckles, and reminiscences. You might even get an old moth-eaten photo fished out of a pocket. This person probably won't have spoken to another soul for days and will see you as a captive audience. If you get an old couple they'll proceed to argue whether it's 100 yards past the post office or 150 yards past the post office, and if, in fact, the post office is still there. Or was it the pub that closed down? What's worse is that they will give you far more instructions than you can ever remember. It's impossible to remember more than four road directions at a time. Like being taken round the building on your first day at work and being introduced to the whole department at once – after about five people they just go in one ear and out the other.

MOTORING ABROAD

France: 'Les Flics' de Vitesse – Speed Police

For a nation that prides itself on how quickly it drives and for whom authority needs to be snubbed at every possible turn, the French put up with some very wily speed police. Not for them the police officer in a high-visibility jacket standing in a conspicuous place, next to a patrol car, waving a gun-like object, with a big flashing neon sign that says "YOU REALISE THERE'S A POLICEMAN WAITING FOR YOU!"

No, the French take it more long-range. Les Flics will station themselves at the end of a very long, straight, quiet piece of road (preferably downhill so even a Renault Twingo can get up to a considerable whack) and use a telescope/radar device to clock you from beneath their camouflaged bivouac.

By the time you see the speed cops it's already too late. Thankfully, the spirit of a nation that stormed the Bastille and ignores most EU rules is alive and well and a helpful van driver will flash you before you arrive on the scene.

France: Zebra Crossings

These are painted on the road in France as a kind of civic duty; a job-creation scheme for local council workers. Nobody has explained to French motorists how they work or what they're for and they are generally ignored. If you go to any tourist town in Northern France and want to find a British car, the easiest way is to stand by a zebra crossing. The first car that stops for you will be a British car.

Similarly, the French don't understand the concept of "letting someone go first" when you could easily get your bumper in front of theirs and keep them trapped in a side road. Cars behind will beep you if you try this more than once. C'est bizarre!

They also don't understand it when you're holding them up in a narrow, winding country lane and move over to let them overtake. Hein? Crazy Anglais! (Sorry Pay de Galles, Pay d'Ecosse and Pay d' Irlande Nord, but unless you're playing rugby you're all collectively Anglais.) You've just given away the lead.

Yours truly once almost got into a fist fight because a French car was blocking the exit to a full car park. I was trying to leave the car park, but the car in front was convinced that someone in front of him was about to move soon. Even though they hadn't turned up to unlock their car. There was no space to move over so he was quite content to sit there and wait and block the exit.

The pièce de résistance of one French holiday was a fire engine trying to get through a line of traffic on a hot August day and cars refusing to move over for it. Obviously there were a lot of people on their way to a restaurant that day.

French Motorways

Ever since the 1960s the French have loved a good movie. But the movie the French love THE best is an American action-drama starring Sandra Bullock, Dennis Hopper and Keanu Reeves – *Speed*. For those who haven't seen it, Sandra Bullock's bus has to keep going at 50 mph or above or it will trigger a bomb that's been placed on board.

Every day on the toll roads of France, French drivers try to emulate this movie. The speed limit of 130 kph (80 mph) on tolls is seen as the minimum speed required – drive anything below it and they will explode wiz ze humiliation of being classed as a slow driver. Even tractors and trailers and road rollers will attempt to overtake you at 80 mph on a *péage*. Take a trip south on the autoroute to the Cote D'Azur or the Alpine skiing resorts and footle along at 75 mph – it feels like you've parked. And it's not all French cars, either. In a bid to create some kind of national identity other than chocolate-making, beer-drinking, that-bit-between-Holland-and-France, the Belgians try and drive even faster than the French. They have the advantage in that unlike their neighbours, they are allowed to buy a car that isn't a Peugeot, a Renault or a Citroën.

Le Deviation

The French are very much into deviation. Now I'm not suggesting that Nicolas and Carla like to dress up as traffic wardens and slap tickets on each other's private parts – that's a given – but they do like to stray off the main route. In France they have no choice. The French departments have a gung-ho approach to road improvement. They'll shut off a major route for six months while they reprofile and resurface it and if you want to use that route – well *tant pis, cherie*.

Whereas in this country we'd have a draft plan, a public consultation, a local inquiry, a planning appeal, an environmental impact assessment, modifications, periods of notice etc., turning a six-month job into a six-year job, the French just do it.

However, as much as I'd like to admire this take-no-prisoners attitude, their ability to signpost deviations are shockingly bad. Just off the main road there'll be the familiar yellow signs for the first three junctions. Then after that… nothing. *Riens du tout*. You're left wandering around the countryside in search of the next deviation sign like a Japanese tourist in the Jubilee Maze. You haven't got a hope in hell of finding the correct exit; you just hope you can latch onto another car that seems to be heading in the same direction.

The Tour de France cycle race helps bring easily-passed-over parts of rural France to the attention of tourists through its meandering course. Badly signposted deviations do it so much better.

Le Spontaneous Roadblock

You know me, I'm not one to trot out national stereotypes, but there's nothing those garlic and cheese-eating surrender monkeys like better than a bit of spontaneous industrial action. Having fought for liberté, égalité and fraternité in 1792 they don't need much of an excuse to get out there and block the national road network for some cause.

It seems that everyone with a big vehicle likes having a go. The fishermen string their boats together and disrupt ferry travel for days on end; the truck drivers place lorries at key road intersections, even the stroppy vegetable farmers join in.

"Les Legumiers Violent" isn't a headline about a bunch of angry courgettes. It's what happens when a bunch of potato farmers get the hump and empty out tonnes of new potatoes on roundabouts in August, because the French government won't buy the vegetable producers' surplus stock. Roundabouts take on the appearance of a fruit and veg department of a large supermarket, there are potatoes everywhere.

If you haven't got a big vehicle to block something, then you have got to go to all the trouble of organising a march in Paris, and that involves mixing with Parisians. So the Premiership of French strikers consists of: fishermen, lorry drivers, farmers and the yet-to-be-properly-organised Union of Quarry Truck Drivers. Train drivers would love to get stuck in, too, but they can't get their engines off the line and park them somewhere inconvenient.

So, motoring through La Belle France you always have to keep one eye open to the possibilities of a lightning strike. Unlike in the UK, where most policemen worth their paycheck will be itching to get the riot gear out and enjoy some lively demonstrator/baton interaction, in France they stand around like a community support officer on their first day in the job.

Continental Truck Drivers

Forget the Galapagos finches, Darwin should have studied the breed that is the continental truck driver. Despite originating from many countries across the mainland of Europe, through time, they have evolved into a single species. They are short, with some kind of moustachio thing going on. They wear vests or cut-off-sleeve T-shirts with red nylon shorts and sandals or flip flops. Even in winter.

To man, this species looks like it should be on some specialist register, and I think we all know what kind of register we're talking about here. Presumably, sending them out on the road for many days at a time lessens the chance of re-offending.

Toll Roads

And talking about toll roads, why is it that if you want to use the decent roads in France you have to pay for the pleasure? Take a trip almost anywhere in Europe by road and you'll end up bolstering the French road-building programme somewhere along the line and it'll cost you a massive £60 in tolls to get anywhere near Italy.

In a way, it's like the EU before Margaret set about them; it's all take, take, take and no give. I would have thought that with the national debt spiralling out of control one of the easiest things would be to quiz all French drivers when they arrive in Dover and Portsmouth and ask them where they'll be going, then slap a bill on them that they have to pay right there and then. That's what they do in Switzerland. When you arrive at the border, the police officer says, "Welcome to Switzerland, are you going to be using the motorway?" And the minute you say you are, they ask you to go to a little office and pay for a sticker that entitles you to drive on an unremarkable two-lane highway. This is actually a good introduction to the miserly, small-minded, Nazi-gold-hoarding nuclearphobes' way of doing business – the Swiss have introduced a charge for everything imaginable, including (as we found in Saas-Fee) walking up mountains. The Von Trapp family were very lucky to have got over the Swiss border from Austria when they escaped in World War II. Had they not had some loose change for two adults and seven children's mountain-hiking passes (high season) that could have been their escape scuppered. Incidentally, ze girl Lisl, if she is over 16 and is going on 17, should pay for the full adult pass.

Alternatively, ban all French and Swiss cars from using The UK's motorways for fear of having their cars impounded and crushed.

Crazy Driving – Malta

Driving in Malta is like Russian Roulette played out in a car. The island isn't big enough to speed in, so by the time you've got your foot to the floor you've arrived at the ferry to Gozo at the top of the island. So, what to do if you're an incorrigible thrill merchant and want to get your kicks behind the wheel? Well, how about driving head-on at each other…or…not slowing down when you get to towns…or…making up the rules of the highway code as you go along. Because that's what you do in Malta. You don't need to know if you give way to vehicles coming from the left, or if you give way to the right. You just don't give way!

In Malta, the driving test consists of switching on the ignition and finding any forward gear. That's it, you've passed. Mirror, signal, manoeuvre? Why complicate things unnecessarily? The correct order is manoeuvre, then signal. If you signal first you've given the game away.

The rear-view mirror is like the human appendix, it's of no real use. It's only there to see what you've just run over and, occasionally, the abusive hand signal used by the driver of a passing car. Oh, and also to see what suspension parts you've just lost after driving over a pothole the size of a goat. Road maintenance is an aspiration not a practice. The life expectancy of a hire vehicle on Malta is rated in hours not years. If the local maniacs don't get you, then the roads will. There is one Lamborghini Countach on the island with a ride height of about 12" between the front spoiler and the road. It's confined to a 120-yard strip of tarmac in Valletta.

Crazy Driving – Macedonia

A friend who has been to Malta and Macedonia says that Macedonia is worse.

Autobahn Driving

The Germans have a Vorsprung Durch Technik reputation for being highly logical and scientific in outlook. They are a teutonic nation that values efficiency and mechanical virtue...except that's all a load of baloney. If that's the case, then why can you drive your car any speed you like on an autobahn instead of the highly efficient 56 mph?

Driving on an autobahn is a novel experience. Cars appear in your wing mirror like they were doing a land speed record attempt. First of all there's a dot in the distance, then suddenly the dot gets very large, very quickly; the blast wave hits your car and, ka-boom, it's gone in the blink of an eye with a throaty exhaust roar. You keep expecting to find bits of Porsche Cayenne splattered across the carriageway a few kilometres down the road – because you need an enormous expanse of tarmac to stop from 140 mph even if you have performance disc brakes (and surely someone's going to be so dumb as to pull out without looking).

When you don't, you realise that it's because everyone has to take autobahns seriously in Michael Schumacher's homeland. Whereas speeds in the UK vary between about 55 mph and 80 mph on the M4, M1 and M8, on an autobahn that difference can potentially be 90 mph and is quite regularly 45 mph. With speed differentials like that you can't cruise down the motorway shouting abuse at Chris Moyles or giving yourself a manicure, safe in the knowledge that nothing much in your world's going to change in the next five or six seconds. On an autobahn you need to pay very close attention to your rear-view mirror. The reason that there aren't mega pile-ups on a regular basis is that people have to concentrate very hard.

Achtung, Baby!

But when they do have pile-ups, they can be spectacular. When a rain shower hit the A2 Autobahn between Hanover and Peine in July 2009 it caused a pile-up that involved 259 cars and injured 60 people. Ultimately, it's no great surprise that the nation with the fastest speed limit in Europe also enjoys the biggest pile-ups. They were all nice cars, too. There's probably a clip doing the rounds on YouTube that looks like a tornado's ripped through a second-hand Mercedes car lot.

Late-Night Petrol

It's rare for us to be leading the field in anything to do with motoring, but I can assure you that we are. Drive across Europe and try to find a petrol station that is open late at night and not on one of the major routes and it's like trying to find a vegetarian in France (one in Marseilles, one in Limoges and one that will eat fish in

Rennes). You can find credit-card-operated pumps at supermarkets that offer you the promise of fuel, then spit out your Visa like it was a Homebase loyalty card. And there's never any chance to pick up a jumbo packet of Maltesers, two AA-sized batteries or 20 Marlboro Light.

The Glorious August 1st

August 1st in France is like the start of a nineteenth-century American land race. The French know the rest of the nation is going to be out there jamming up the same roads, but like Gauloises-smoking lemmings, the pack instinct takes over; they load up the car, pile on the bicyclettes and they're off. Nobody thinks to themselves, "Actuellement, I'm going to save myself a lot of pain and distress and go the day after," that is not the French way. So, come the day of the annual migration, the roads are a total nightmare, locked solid from 7 a.m. to 10 p.m. Most horrendous of all, they are jammed up between 12 a.m. and 2 p.m., when every self-respecting French motorist should be in a restaurant and not sitting in a queue. The traffic news goes bonkeurs. Every year, the highest death toll on French roads occurs on August 1st, prompting one heretical French government aide to suggest that the French should drive more like the British. Well, I can tell you pal, the British would stagger their journeys. And they wouldn't drive in vests with track-suit bottoms, or carry man bags into service stations either.

CAR "CHARACTERS"

For a long while now people have been using the word "character" as a euphemism. "He's a bit of a character" isn't a phrase laden with reverence or affection, it's another way of saying "nutter". The guy who spends an afternoon sitting in his boot with a Haynes manual in one hand trying to work out how to replace a bulb in his offside rear-light cluster is not a character, he's a nutter. That's what garages are for. The boys at J&P Motors could sort it all out in about 57 seconds, but no, some people will insist on doing it themselves, doing it slowly and doing it badly. Or perhaps they want to create "alternative" cars. Perhaps Vauxhall missed a trick by not putting the rear-light clusters in upside down.

This section is dedicated to various motoring "characters" who illuminate and enhance our enjoyment of everyday life by making us think – there by the grace of God go I. As Mr Bennet says in *Pride and Prejudice*, what are our neighbours for if not to make sport for us? Though in Jane Austen's day they didn't have such a developed concept of institutional care, even if they did have "pimp my barouche".

Krooklok Guy

This is a man who has no idea how little his car is worth. Either that or he can't bear the thought of anyone getting behind the wheel of his beloved vehicle apart from him. How does he protect his little beauty from the wolves out there that are just waiting to pounce with a screwdriver and a bent bit of wire?

With a Krooklok, that's how.

What kind of cars are protected by that ultimate of Krook deterrents? A new BMW 7 series, a Mercedes SLK, or perhaps a Bentley Continental?

No. Try a seven-year-old Rover 55. There is a legion of men out there driving ridiculously un-fanciable cars who think that by adding a Krooklok their cars become Fort Knox on wheels. My father-in-law once drove an MG Metro worth £650, for which he needed a £700 service. Which meant that the Krooklok was actually worth more than the car.

If Smigal from *Lord of the Rings* had a car, he would buy a Krooklok for it.

And the fantastic irony is that most competent criminals can unlock Krookloks in less than thirty seconds. So all you're doing is providing a challenge, a kind of Rubik's Cube mental stimulation for the thief to puzzle out before he nicks your car anyway. The kind of people who can't undo them are junior joyriders learning their trade. So they should be called Youf-loks, not Krookloks.

Classic-Car Guy

This is a man with two garages for whom regular sex is no longer an option. After spending a fortune on tickets to musicals like *Mamma Mia!* and many nights in Harvester restaurants, he has finally given up on getting his leg over. So, instead of lavishing attention on his wife, he has decided to fulfil a childhood dream and buy a car he once had as a Top Trump.

It might be a Jaguar like Morse's, it could be an old MGA or a modern classic like a Datsun 240Z, but the relationship is always the same. A great-looking classic car is like a trophy wife. He wants to get out there and be seen with her/it.

Though he thinks it makes him look interesting – perhaps a little intriguing, especially if he buys an old convertible and a WWII flying jacket – he's wrong. The only people who are remotely interested are fellow classic car enthusiasts. To the opposite sex it's an old car that's been polished a lot. Most women are not fluent in "car" and put vehicles into vague categories such as big, sporty, flash, people-carrier-ish, 4x4, new, old, small, tiny, long, high, blue. Or they create a whole new category that men can't relate to – my wife came up with "lesbian librarian-ish" (she was talking about a VW Polo, in case you're wondering).

It's not just a physical relationship either: rubbing, touching, stroking, buffing. Classic cars have a certain nostalgic smell to them. When Classic-Car Guy gets onboard he's regressing back to a simpler world, a time before complex financial derivatives, a time when he had more hair, more sex appeal and there was a heady optimism that things would turn out better than they actually did.

He keeps his car in one half of a double garage, which means that the other half is piled high with rubbish. His wife and children despair of having to creep round it and live in fear of leaving a bike resting against the holy icon.

Each year he'll make a journey to Mecca where he can worship with fellow believers. His pilgrimage – ringed conspicuously in the diary the moment the newsletter comes out – to the annual Triumph/MG/Jaguar/Hillman/Owner's Club rally held at an airfield or agricultural showground, is the highlight of his year. There he can bore the bollocks off fellow owners about the time he found an interesting bit of chrome trim that matched the radiator grill. Except, of course, they won't be bored, they'll be enthralled. Sad bastards.

Car-Cleaning Man

Like the man who insists on doing his own vehicle repairs, there are people out there who insist on cleaning their own cars every week. What is the point of the expanded EU if it's not to give jobs to Bulgarian hand car washers? You pay £10, drive in, they wash your car, it's done. It's a much better solution than those clanky car cleaning machines that rip off your bumper, your aerial, your wing mirrors and leave your car aerodynamically improved, but accessory free.

The alternative is to waste two hours of a Sunday when you could be reading the newspapers, hitting a golf ball, watching sport or simply down the pub.

Car-Cleaning Man has no demands on his time whatsoever. He's a tidy, fussy obsessive, the kind of guy who loves routine. He will wash his car the same way, with the same cloth procedure, the same application of chamois leather, Turtle Wax, Simoniz, etc. At the end of it, he will stand back and think, "My car is in showroom condition." But if it's a Kia Sorento, all it is is a Kia Sorento in showroom condition.

You could maybe understand it if the car were an eye-popping Audi A8, or a Ford GT40 replica, or a muscle-bound AC Cobra. Because then it would be like a true act of worship for a bit of modern automotive art. But not if it's a Toyota Camry 1.8.

If there is one good thing about a water shortage or a hosepipe ban, it's knowing that Car-Cleaning Man is going to be driven insane by the boulders of dirt that his car has picked up over seven days' road usage.

Haynes-Manual Man

Only a couple of chromosomes away from Car-Cleaning Man and Classic-Car Guy is Haynes-Manual Man. These are the kind of men who love a mechanical challenge and have the patience of Job, and also a Haynes manual. Like Classic-Car Guy they have long given up the hope of any kind of sexual encounter, outside of anniversaries and drunkenness, and have dedicated themselves to their car's wellbeing.

Their garages are a recreation of a main dealer's service department, with the concrete floor painted grey and a line demarking the ideal spot where the car should be parked within. They dream of installing their own car lift, but of course that would mean going up through the ceiling into the guest bedroom and would probably shatter the uneasy truce that exists between himself and the good lady. At the moment she is still prepared to launder three sets of grey mechanics overalls which are kept in readiness (one for best, one for reserve and one for oil changes).

On the wall of his pristine garage are an arsenal of tools, each with an assigned space and a profile on the wall denoting where they should go – thus making it immediately conspicuous if required tool is missing.

Addiction to the Haynes manual is a sign of buttock-clenching anality or banality, whichever way you want to look at it. It is their bible and it is followed relgiously. If the writers of Haynes manuals wanted to throw in a couple of joke instructions; like every four hours turning towards Dagenham and offering a prayer to the God "Henry", they would be followed implicitly.

The diligence and respect shown to these guides means that any simple job can take between five and ten times the man hours it would take a trained mechanic to complete the task. What's more, as cars have become more sophisticated and high-tech, the equipment needed to do a lot of the specialist jobs is not available to the enthusiastic amateur.

Though having said that, Haynes produced a manual for the Citroën GS in the 1970s, a car so ridiculously overcomplicated that changing a front suspension part meant removing the engine.

Coned-Off-Parking-Space Man (or Woman)

Unlike the above, this is not a single-sex trait. These people are amongst some of the most irritating gits you are likely to come across on God's earth. Whereas we can smile at Haynes-Manual Man and give him a friendly wave, if you live next door to Coned-Off-Parking-Space Man or Woman, murder is never far off your mind.

These people live in tight, terraced roads, or where there is a high concentration of Victorian or Edwardian semis. They are of the opinion that they own the bit of road outside their house and no one else should be allowed to park there. When they go out, they block the road for two minutes while positioning cones in the space they have just left. They are not expecting a delivery, they're just expecting to park right where they want to when they come back.

Should anyone have the bottle to put the traffic cones onto the pavement and park in the space, they will come back to find a furious note on their windscreen citing asthma, arthritis, constant back-breaking deliveries, etc., that make the cones necessary and accusing you of being evil, uncaring spawn of the devil.

If this doesn't work, then the level of intimidation is cranked up to aerials being mysteriously bent overnight, scrapes on the side of the car, tyres becoming unusually flat. In the end, it is just easier to avoid them.

Buddhists have identified the trait as being part of the human condition. It is, they reason, part of the human condition to always want more, and to always be irked by someone parking in front of your house. We work hard to suppress these twin feelings of negativity and only become truly happy when there is an abundance of parking space.

Coned-Off-Parking-Space Man's kama can be tested on two levels. The first is to move his traffic cones the second he is gone and allow some wholly innocent motorist to occupy the spot. The second is best attempted during the winter months when it gets dark early. Under the cover of darkness it is much easier to sneak out and steal the cones and find a loving home for them in a skip four roads away. This means that COPSM/W has to find a constant source of new cones to support his/her habit.

The Mercedes Family

I don't profess to be a qualified psychologist, but a family whose members all have to drive Mercedes has BIG problems. It's a status symbol thing. If you don't have a Mercedes you're letting the family down. You don't see families where everyone insists on driving a Renault, or everyone rocks up to a family event in a range of different Fiats or a phalanx of Vauxhalls.

Dad wants to impress and buys a top-of-the-range Merc. His brother then has to compete, so he buys one as well. Dad has to go one better and buys a smaller A or B-Class for his wife – now his brother has to go one better and get an AMG-styled, souped-up version, making him the alpha male of the family. As soon as their sons and daughters reach driving age, they have to have Mercedes, too. Maybe even a Smart car. Parking for family events look like someone's emptied out the forecourt of a local Mercedes garage.

Lexus, Audi, BMW and Porsche produce cars that are better than many of the Mercedes models, but when you're part of a Mercedes Family, then they might as well be dog carts.

Roof-Rack Man

Remember the refrain from the They Might Be Giants song... "Roof-rack man, Roof-rack man; has no need, to hire a van"?

The reason he doesn't need to hire a van is because he can get everything on his roof rack ("the best investment I ever made"). Roof-Rack Man laughs at the suggestion he'd try and get the kitchen sink on his roof rack, because he's had it up there many times before, together with a variety of different IKEA kitchen units and a Whirlpool integrated dishwasher. He is an ergonomic genius, knowing just how much he can stuff inside of his car and on top of his car without attracting police attention, or toppling over sideways. He has suitable ropes and bungee chords to "facilitate" the task.

His loving partner never worries about packing too much when they go away on holiday because she knows that Roof-Rack Man will accommodate it. True, they might have to drive to Northern Spain at 36 mph because of the massive wind resistance of the seven trunks on the roof, but she won't be short of evening wear choices.

The complete opposite of Roof-Rack Man is IKEA-Car-Park-Despair Man. This is someone who has merrily purchased a range of different items from the Swedish furniture giant and got back to his car to find that only three of them will fit. At which point, there is much teeth gnashing and tearing of hair and accusations of buying that Splürghølm or the Krøggflutt they really didn't need.

The wife and I once met a man with two mattresses on a trolley looking forlornly at his Mercedes sports car in the IKEA Croydon car park. "I forgot I was in this car," was all he could say.

Old-Banger Dealer

This is a man who's looking for a bit of extra income by doing up old cars that were otherwise heading down the dumper. With insurance write-offs based on the high labour costs billed by main dealers and brand new replacement parts, many old cars can be written off for really tiny jobs.

Old-Banger Dealer rescues these vehicles, does the repairs himself using second-hand parts from scrapyards, and, hey presto, the car's ready to be advertised in the local paper. Given that the carbon footprint for producing a new car is massive compared to maintaining an old one, Banger Dealer is an eco warrior.

Banger Dealer's front garden is easy to spot. There will be as many old cars there as can be fitted into the space, bumper to rusting bumper. One, with some of its windows missing, will be under an old tarpaulin. He will have a generous array of sheds in his back garden, all full of parts of cars that aren't needed for now, but are too valuable to throw away. There will be a rich smell of oil and rust, and the cars will be surrounded by various wheels, tyres, old towbars, bumpers and wings.

Though he intends to have the cars out the front for just a couple of weeks, most of them eventually dissolve into the subsoil before he gets round to doing something about them.

His hands are invariably black and his aftershave is Eau de Swarfega.

People living next to Old-Banger Dealer despise him, until the morning they are late for a meeting and their car won't start.

Scalextric Man

Scalextric Man doesn't own a Scalextric set – the enduringly popular racing game, with 1/32 scale model sports cars that race round a track (where one lane is clearly a lot faster than the other) is of no interest to this driver. Who is a complete and pant-filling liability.

A short trip as a passenger with Scalextric Man is more scary than a lap of Silverstone with Lewis Hamilton or a rally stage with Marcus Grönholm. Yet the finger-gnawing journey does not take place on a race track or a forest rally stage.

Scalextric Man drives down any road like it was a Scalextric track. He believes the white line down the centre of the road is like the electric pick-up, thus he straddles the line, placing half his car on the right side of the road and half on the less-sympathetic-to-oncoming-traffic side of the road.

He is scared stiff of parked cars and would sooner have a head-on collision with an oncoming vehicle than risk the tiniest brush against anything on his side of the road. When it comes to overtaking push bikes, he needs at least 3 metres of clearance before he'll go past. Horses? Don't even bother, he waits behind them till they return to their stables.

You can often recognise Scalextric Man by a lack of wing mirror on the driver's side, or by his partner, who will have turned prematurely grey. Equip him with a long enough caravan and he could gridlock a decent-sized county.

Dogmobile Couple

Dogmobile Couple's day revolves around taking the dog for a walk. Sometimes two. They may be childless, or their children may have grown up and left home, but now they devote all their time and attention to the dog. Dogmobile Couple favour Volvos and Honda CRVs, with the rear section grilled off and entirely devoted to the much-loved pooch. They will have installed a special basket with blanket, provided a reassuring chewy toy, plus there will be all the paraphernalia of dog walking; leads, leashes, a towel, a pooper scooper, spare pooper scooper, scoop bags, a bowl for those thirsty moments in summer, perhaps a coat for the chilly walks in winter, all stashed neatly away. When Doggie gets a little bit old and infirm they have a folding ramp that he can walk up to get in. Were Honda to offer the option of a tail-lift for dogs on their CRV then Dogmobile Couple would seriously consider it.

Dogmobile Couple need to have two cars, otherwise whenever they go anywhere, people will ask, "What's that awful doggie smell?" and they'll have to confess, "Ermmm...that must be us."

WHEN GOOD CARS GO BAD

Main-Dealer Servicing

Having your car serviced by a main dealer is always a battle of wits. Dealers across the whole spectrum of cars – budget to luxury – operate a system that is very close to legalised fraud. It is the motorist's job to sniff out the essential repairs from the non-essential repairs. For many of us, it's the only opportunity we have to play Rumpole of the Bailey and cross-examine a very slippery witness in the dock.

Here's what happens – and it's no different from Ford to Mercedes. You drop your car in for service. Two hours later at work you get a call from the service manager detailing a shopping list of additional work you'll need doing, that's apart from your £150 service. His strategy is to mix up the must-be-done jobs with the cosmetic niceties so you think they all have the same degree of urgency. Your job is to ask him questions that expose his extra jobs as nothing more than nice little earners for the garage. One of the greatest "little extras" was tried on by Mercedes who wanted to add "summer coolant" to the radiator for the price of £50. They didn't have any luck there.

Other garages like to throw in items such as "worn suspension bushes", which is always a good one because it sounds significant. When you say to them, yes, but I'd like to keep the old ones to make sure they're sufficiently worn, there is often silence. They will parry with, "We recommend that it is done," which you have to counter with, "will I need it to pass the MOT?"

Main dealers are very keen to change stuff earlier than necessary, as this typical exchange bears out:

Garage: The brake pads are 80 per cent gone.
Me: So there's 20 per cent left.
Garage: Yes, but we recommend you change them now.
Me: I have a brake warning light, surely that will tell me when they need to be changed.
Garage: We wouldn't recommend that.
Me: Then why have the light?
Garage: It's more like a failure light.

A good habit to get into is to insist any old part that the garage has replaced be left in a box in your boot. That sharpens their mind on what is worn out or not. My 80 per cent worn-out brake pads have lasted two years.

Not content with making your warranty invalid unless you have your car serviced by them, they like to wag their finger about dealer recommendations. The implication being that if you don't follow their recommendation you are taking a BIG RISK. There's always the risk that my car is going to be car-jacked unless I hire a former member of the SAS to sit in the back armed with an automatic weapon, but, you know, I'm just going to take that risk.

Speedy Fit Tyre and Kwik Exhausts

You don't need to be a high-powered retail analyst to work out you're standing in the reception of Speedy Fit Tyres and Kwik Exhausts.

You can be robbed of your sense of smell and your sense of hearing, but as long as you can see that cash register, you know where you are. Because it will be grimy charcoal black. This signature filth theme is continued in the toilets, where the basins are also filthy black. It's fair to say that coal miners emerging from a 10-hour shift underground could maintain premises better than Speedy Fit Tyres and Kwik Exhausts.

The idea of Speedy Fit Tyres and Exhausts is to get you up on a ramp, problem diagnosed and back on the road as soon as possible. It's a good concept, if you have one of the ten most common cars in the UK. If you don't, then it's a case of, "We don't stock that as standard, but we can order it in." They then expect you to wait around for about three hours in a reception area whose comfort level is on a par with an Eastern Bloc prison from the 1970s.

Even when it's a simple job, say a punctured front tyre, everyone seems to get served before you do.

Barry the Mechanic

Irritating people are always telling me that if I had a car like theirs, I could take it to Barry the Mechanic and save myself a fortune. Barry the Mechanic (not his real name) used to work for a big garage, but now he's started up on his own, working from a little lock-up under the arches. These people are keen to tell you that he knows far more about their car than any other person and charges a fraction of what they used to pay.

This is fine, until a few years down the line Barry the Mechanic fails to recognise the symptoms of a split piston ring and the engine eats itself going north on the M1 with damage to the tune of three thousand smackers. I never believe people who crow about how little they pay for servicing. If someone is that good then it's best to keep sshtumm.

Accident Weasels

These are the people who are deeply regretful to your face after they've run into you, but change their story and attitude the minute they leave the scene. Weasels. For this reason, keep a camera in your car and, providing you're not in imminent danger of being run over by a lorry, take a picture of the accident before any vehicles are moved. Take it before you've even talked to the other person, sorry, weasel. With the exception of the doctor who knocked me off my pushbike while going through a red light and turning right against a no-right-turn sign, everyone who's ever hit me has turned into a weasel the minute they've left the scene.

Late-Night Tow Truckers

They came from out of the seething Mathmos – late-night tow truckers. On an evolutionary scale they are somewhere between the Hunchback of Notre Dame and a cave troll, but one that has equipped itself with a driving licence and a tow-truck (kept in the cave). They emerge out of the darkness at speed, like some head-of-the-food-chain predator, and reverse up to your stricken vehicle. They are the strong, silent, hairy-knuckled type, uttering few words and as many grunts in their summary loading of your car. They're not great on small talk during your fretful journey home, which is good.

If you could put aside the shameless itching of unmentionable places, the ghoulish references to other cars they've picked up and a tendency to belch, they are nice guys. But it's good for everyone they work nights.

AA Men

In contrast, AA Men are remorselessly cheerful and won't allow you to wallow in the slough of despond you want to slide into after your car breaks down. You want to bitch and moan, but they remain steadfastly optimistic. Their theme tune should be "always look on the bright side of life". They have smart vans, equipment that works and have the demeanour of people trained at The Samaritans. They are non-judgemental, too. You can do the most ridiculously stupid thing to your car and not a flicker of "what a total wally" will pass their countenance when you tell them. You can drain the battery using an in-car refrigerator, leave the handbrake on too lightly and watch it roll into a pond, or lock your keys inside and it will always be a total delight to help you out.

But if Green Flag are cheaper, I use them.

USELESS THINGS

Car Insurance Company Adverts

Car insurance companies are responsible for some of the worst adverts ever to be screened on British television. Elephant, Admiral, Esure and every price comparison website, with the exception of the meerkats, produce the kind of intellectual stimulation that makes watching paint dry a pleasure. Over-expose yourself to these adverts and you'll need to check yourself into the nearest intensive care unit and stick your brain on an EEG to see if there's anything left.

The adverts are full of grinning fatheads who gurn inanely at the camera: "I saved myself £150 on my car insurance!" Yes, because you told them it was a Ford Ka and not a left-hand drive Nissan Skyline GT with heavily modified carburettors and non-standard inlet manifolds.

Presumably, these are the same people that shop extensively the day before major sales and need to be told that the large metal grill at the edge of the pavement isn't a savings bank, it's a drain.

Bemused.com

Insurance comparison websites, they're great aren't they? No, they're not. Well, yes they are, providing you don't want anything too radical. I filled out an online form over what seemed like three days for Bemused.com. They certainly wanted a lot of detail. And if I got a bit bored and skipped a couple of questions, they wouldn't let me. No, I had to tell them everything; the name of my daughter's first school, my preference for marmalade over honey as a breakfast conserve, the colour of the vehicle that in the event of an accident I might like to drive (providing the accident wasn't my fault and it wasn't within 500 metres of my house). At the end of all that they went away to consider the best quote possible for me...and came up with nothing. It wasn't as though I was trying to insure something a bit specialist – like a left-hand drive Chevrolet Corvette or an amphibious vehicle – it was a diesel Ford Mondeo.

Pimp My Grump

Occasionally, when I'm channel hopping on the box, a misplaced digit will find me at *Pimp My Ride*. I'm sure Lord Reith never imagined a broadcasting world where we would have programmes called *Pimp My Ride* clogging up the airwaves. If this kind of trendy expression spread to the rest of television it would be anarchy – *Gardener's World* would become *Pimp My Shed*, *Antiques Roadshow* would become, *'Sho Looks Old, Baby* and the news would become *Yo, Wass Happenin'*?

In *Pimp My Ride*, they take a knackered old shell of a vehicle that's best left to the crusher and spend enough money to buy three new models, turning it into a tart's boudoir-come-discotheque on wheels.

The opiate of the people is *Max Power*, a publication that you can find distressingly more easily than my old stalwart *Motorsport Monthly*. Inside, you'll find motors with women in reduced clothing circumstances draped all over them, as though they have been pulled there by magnets attached to their bra straps.

In fact, I'm aware of a particularly distasteful phrase referring to a car as a "_____ magnet", once told to me by a 24-hour vehicle recovery driver. Referring to my Vauxhall Omega, which had been strapped onto his truck, he opined, "It's not exactly a _____ magnet, is it?" Mercifully, Mrs Grump was engaged in finding the apostrophe for a text she was sending.

It may be a trusty workhorse, but it's one Vauxhall Omega that won't be decked out in 4" neon green shagpile all over the interior and have enough speakers to broadcast the farewell concert of Kanye West (whoever that is).

Body-Styling Kits

We have an amiable nutter who lives at the bottom of the road who is forever outside tinkering with his venerable Mark 3 Ford Cortina. The car is worth £30 or less and the bodywork looks like it's 25 per cent Ford original and 75 per cent Polyfilla. But he's happy as Eeyore with his balloon, filling and sanding and painting, and painting and sanding and filling, in a pair of overalls that look like they came supplied with the car in 1976. If he ever gave up lavishing so much time on such a pointless occupation people would start to worry.

It must be the same set of human genes that make men in their twenties and thirties spend £15,000 on "improving" a Citroën Saxo by bolting on new wheel arches, a chrome-plated exhaust and sticking ultra-violet lights underneath. What is the point of those then? Is it an attempt by young men to provide a much-needed under-car disco environment for hedgehogs? There are many contenders for Most Pointless Addition to a Great Car (and those who watched *Jamie's Italy* on television would agree that the most useless addition to a Volkswagen Camper was Jamie Oliver) but a disco light shining down on tarmac underneath the car has got to be way up there.

The sum total of all these "kick ass" improvements in your "ICE", your "body styling" and your "rubber and rims", is a massive bill and a new insurance group that puts you on a par with a stunt driver who drives to work on two wheels with his car ablaze. And at the end of the day you haven't got a Maserati, have you? It's still a Citroën Saxo.

4x4s

Personally, I blame Princess Anne for all this. It's her love of Land Rovers that has cascaded down the classes and made every suburban mum with an infant at prep school anxious to have a big solid status symbol to take their little darling to school every morning.

And they're so, so, so right to. Lurking in every leafy suburb is an evil bulldozer, or similar large tonnage track-laying vehicle, ready to crush a standard four-door saloon on its way to school, like it was Billy Goat Gruff. No way could it handle a 4x4, that can pass on its way.

Thus a vehicle that is built to travel up a 1 in 3 incline on a tricky loose-shale surface, spends its life on flat urban tarmac dreaming of getting just a little bit muddy. Cars that are built to tackle mountains rarely have more than a sleeping policeman to climb up.

It's one of the most absurd cases of capability over use. The one thing that makes me laugh a grumpy laugh more than the fleet of BMWs, Porsches, Mercedes and Range Rovers dropping off Flossy, Cissy, Cuthbert and Roderick outside posh schools is the army of commuters who go to work in bush-ranger coats. These jackets are thorn-proof and designed for Australian backwoodsmen, yet Nigel in Finance clearly believes that the hostile environment of the 8.10 a.m. from Surbiton merits dressing up like Crocodile Dundee.

The Porsche Cayenne is perhaps the supreme example of man's automotive stupidity. If you want to pay £75,000 for a badly styled Range Rover to taxi the kids to school then a Porsche dealer will happily take your money. It's rare for me to cast newt enthusiast and whiskey lover Ken Livingstone in a saintly light, but his idea about taxing urban 4x4s to the hilt was a real Grump vote winner.

Eco Cars

Almost as bad as gas-guzzling 4x4s are the "eco friendly" hybrid cars. Their owners have a faintly saintly air about them. "We're saving the planet because we've got a Toyota Prius. And, hey, it's great because Cameron Diaz, Gwyneth Paltrow and Leonardo DiCaprio have got one too."

Bunch of old socks! The real way to save the planet is not to buy a new car at all but keep an old one running without emitting clouds of smoke when you change gear. So many earth resources go into making a new car that will never be recouped by the slight improvement in the carbon that's being chucked out the back.

What helps sell the Prius is that it is so badly styled people think it has to be virtuous in some way. It's the motoring equivalent of a nun. Obviously the bloke who designed the Motability scooter had a couple of free lunch hours and decided to knock up the Prius for a giggle.

Paul McCartney got a hybrid Lexus (which is basically a posh Toyota for the Hyacinth Bouquets of this world) from the company so he could be green. The only problem is that the Japanese flew it to him by plane, thus increasing the carbon footprint by about 100 times. Somebody gleefully calculated that it was the same as driving the car round the world six times.

As a footnote, when I mentioned to Mrs Grump that Paul McCartney was going green, she replied that, "It's probably better than the hair colour he's got now."

Personalised Number Plates

I have nothing against personalised number plates. Sometimes the cheeky and inventive combination of letters and numbers can put a smile on your face. That is, if you're short of a few chromosomes.

Seriously, I have nothing against personalised number plates because the DVLA keep all the good ones and flog them off for the benefit of the taxpayer. So, if you're stupid and vain enough to want one, you can shell out an extortionate amount of money for the pleasure. But to my mind they don't go far enough.

The standard format is: area code, age identifier, and the three random letters. But if you want, you can stick on your own highly priced registration number, such as MAG1C.

Why not auction words from the English dictionary instead, so you can go round driving with DAISEY on your car or MOOSE or HAIRY. You could get a stack of cash for all proper words and it's not without precedent. There's an Englishman who drives round California with BOLLOCKS as his licence plate because the Americans don't know what that means.

Furry Dice

I've always wondered about the mental state of anybody with a set of furry dice dangling from their rear-view mirror. For many years I thought it might be some kind of secret signal; perhaps a marker to anyone with another set of furry dice dangling. You know, a bit like the handkerchief-in-the-back-pocket signal. It could have been translated as, "I'm up for a bit of dogging, woof!" or "Let's go somewhere and play snakes and ladders."

Then I thought, perhaps they're used ironically by university professors, who have extended the irony to owning a 10-year-old Toyota Celica and dressing in capped-sleeve T-shirts. But, no, nothing like that. They're just furry dice. All they do is interfere with your vision and make road accidents more likely. They indicate that at home on the sideboard there may well be a collector's edition pottery version of classic moments from *Only*

Fools and Horses, limited to 5,000 pieces signed by the artist and advertised in the *Sunday Express*. Beautiful.

Furry anything in a car is not warranted. Furry seats, furry parcel shelf, furry steering wheel, furry dice. Unless you're a member of The Banana Splits, and that limits in-car furriness to Fleegle, Bingo, Drooper and Snorky, and it's a while since I've seen one of their dune buggies on the North Circular.

Cars that Flash One Another

I don't ever remember taking hallucinogenic drugs and going out and buying a car, but something must have possessed me to buy a Citroën 2CV when I was younger. What you got, apart from a dashboard-mounted gearchange that had a similar motion to sawing wood, and combined wind and engine noise that made conversation in the front seat a bit like bellowing to a friend on the wing of a 747, was people who flashed you.

Actually, not any random people, other 2CV drivers. In the spirit of, "Hey, isn't this fun, we're both driving 2CVs, isn't that marvellous." It might have been okay if they were square-jawed blokes you could share a pint with, or blonde catwalk models keen to discuss the mysteries of the tatty fold-back roof, but no. They were the kind of people that bought llama farmer hats, grew ginger beards and had hobbies such as rug-weaving and went camping in Wales. I didn't really want to be sucked into all that. I hadn't bought into the lifestyle, I had bought into the fact that I had no cash and the 600cc engine used the least amount of fuel with the exception of a Fiat 500 and a Vespa.

Rear Spoilers

The addition of a rear spoiler to a car for driving in the UK is about as useful as adding a pile of LPs to your roof and then driving off. Which I have done. Spoilers are the equivalent of a go-faster stripe or chequered flag stickers. In fact, the stripe and the stickers are better in that they don't introduce drag to your car, which a spoiler does. Spoilers only help if you're a presenter on one of those mindless TV car programmes and have to hurl your vehicle round a bend to prove to your fellow testosterone-deficient road testers that you can shag a set of tyres while still keeping a car on the road. They're not useful for sensible driving.

Spoilers are only there to make the car LOOK faster. Those maddeningly efficient Germans have long scorned Das Spoiler. To prove it, the spoilers on some Porsche sportscars are retractable and only appear when the car hits 75 mph. And only then to boost the driver's ego.

My pile of LPs helped keep my car's rear end glued to the end of the road where the amazed look of a passer by alerted me to the fact that I might have forgotten something.

Hubcaps

Man has come a long way since the invention of the wheel. Newton worked out gravity. Darwin has sorted out natural selection. Einstein has proffered his theory of relativity. We have driven vehicles at the speed of sound, propelled them with solar energy, even taken them to drive on other planets. Man has set himself a series of automotive challenges and come out trumps. But can we get a hubcap-retaining clip to retain a sodding hubcap...? There they lie at the side of every urban dual carriageway; sad, anonymous, forgotten, chipped, bent. They are a dismal reminder that the merest brush of a kerb will have them part company with the wheel to which they were formerly attached.

It's all part of a shocking conspiracy. Go to any franchise dealer and ask the cost of a replacement hubcap and it's one of those "How much...?" moments. "You are joking, aren't you? That price you just quoted me was in Turkish lira, wasn't it...?"

I don't know what it is about hubcaps but the minute you lose one your car looks ****. The car manufacturers know this and design deliberately faulty hubcap-retaining clips in order to recoup millions from spare parts. They are in league with the alloy wheel suppliers who want you to upgrade and buy the latest five-pot alloys.

Adding a Roofrack

One of the many ways you can make a beautifully designed car look like a refugee from *Scrapheap Challenge* is by fitting it with a roofrack. Non-standard ones from Halfords are the best for robbing your car of any aesthetic quality it might have had. The only exception to this rule is the Nissan Almera, where a roofrack is a pleasant distraction to the pile of junk that sits underneath.

Adding a Towbar

A great way of shedding your car's second-hand value is by having a towbar fitted. The minute that prospective buyers see a towbar they immediately assume you've been using your car to tow traction engines to steam rallies, or caravans the size of a small bungalow. And they're right. On the road you see cars lumbering along with yachts, their suspensions loaded down, the back axles being torn out as they lumber up a 1 in 5 gradient. Yet these vehicles never appear for sale in advertisements. The ones advertised in *Auto Trader* universally agree that they have only been used "occasionally", or on light trailers, or on tiny, tiny boats made of gossamer and balsa wood.

Loud Stereos in Cars

As you have seen from the mild reflections on these pages, I am the very last person to stereotype anyone. But when it comes to loud music in cars... it's always a certain kind, isn't it? On a warm summer's evening when you're out for a pleasant stroll, you don't get Mercedes Benz cruising past pumping out the *Ride of the Valkyries* from Wagner's Ring Cycle or Dame Joan Sutherland giving *The Nun's Chorus* full chat from the Vienna Opera House. Pulling up at the traffic lights, your attention isn't grabbed by the incessant pounding of Rufus Wainwright or Duffy. Neither is it Waylon Jennings, The Smiths or Coldplay...it's always drum and bass, the musical equivalent of a road drill. Thud, thud, thud, thud, thud, thud, thud, thud.

Why bother with interrogation techniques, such as waterboarding, when suspected militants could be put in a room with Radio One's Westwood show for two hours. Clearly people who are afflicted by the condition "drum and bass" can't survive in a small space unless drum and bass is being pumped at them at maximum volume all the time, like keeping a dolphin wet or a fish supplied with oxygen.

Outside of the car, they must slip their headphones on immediately for fear that the ghastly chasm of silence and birdsong will engulf them. What fascinates me is the prospect of them growing old in 50 years' time and maybe disappearing down the garden to their drum and bass shed. "Grandad has been playing his funny old music again."

Of course, he'll have gone deaf years before that.

Sun Roofs

I have a theory on sun roofs – their day is over. The sun roof is a child of the 1970s, when package holidays first came to the masses and people realised they could spend a miserable two weeks in Torremolinos almost as cheaply as a miserable two weeks in Llandudno. The big difference was that you could get a suntan in Torremolinos whereas the most exotic thing you could get from Llandudno was a donkey bite or a strange venereal disease from an encounter in the public toilets.

Suddenly, we fell in love with the sun. We wanted more of it, even while motoring. So the car manufacturers came up with a device that would allow us more sun, and ironically, at the same time, more rain, when it started to leak, as it always would do. Especially the ones that didn't have that badge of authenticity: "factory fitted". Apart from being a new ecosystem for mould to colonise, they would also have a tendency to jam open, jam closed, and jam half-open.

Since the birth of the sun roof, a lot more convertible cars have come on the market and while in the 1970s it was just Citroën Dyanes, MGBs and Austin Healeys, in the 80s and 90s we got Volkswagen Golf convertibles, the

Mazda MX5, Peugeot 205 cabriolets. Yes, we became far more chic in the 1980s with our Sade and Matt Bianco records, sipping cappuccino in front of our brand-new Renault cabriolet.

This spelled the end of a titchy square vent that would make people sitting in the back seat uncomfortable and create such wind noise that listening to the car stereo became like tuning in to the British Home Service. These days air conditioning comes as standard and we're all so paranoid about catching skin cancer that even hitch-hikers carry SPF 50 suncream in case they have to accept a lift in a convertible.

And Llandudno has never looked better.

How's My Driving?

You see them on the back of courteously driven lorries, the "How's My Driving?" sign. They are a self-fulfilling prophecy, because inviting criticism only puts drivers on their best behaviour. Added to that they're on lorries run by big corporate names like Tesco and Sainsbury, who are very keen to maintain a good public profile. Where they really should have them is on the back of buses and coaches. Bus drivers have come a long way since the lovable Reg Varney was tootling through the suburbs in his daily duel with Blakey the inspector. These days Reg's successors are mollycoddled novices. They have special bus lanes to cruise down and wander in and out of. They have special instructions in the highway code – fail to let one out when it's indicating and you can fail your driving test. Yet still they're short of anyone with discernible driving talent whose eyesight and vision is on par with a healthy adult mole. Part of the aptitude test for bus drivers is to show them a video of a street scene and see if they can recognise a cyclist in high-visibilty fluorescent clothing. Failure to notice them is an instant pass.

Car Handbooks

When you've paid a gazillion pounds for a brand-new car, the least you can expect is a handbook that refers to your car. But no, what you get is a vague document written for every blinkin' conceivable variant of that car; the two-door version, the four-door version, the five-door hatchback, the estate, the long-wheelbase, the 1.8 litre, the 2.0, the 2.2, the 2.2i 16-valve, the 2.5 turbo diesel and the 3 litre engine that nobody bought.

Look up how to refill the windscreen washer bottle and you will be directed to the wrong part of the engine compartment. After which, you unscrew the radiator top-up reservoir and scald your hand. Having tried several times to work out where the fuses were on the car (an attempt similar to finding priestholes in a manor house, but marginally more high-tech), with the aid of my handbook, I gave up and handed the job over to

J&P Motors. They cheerily gave me the handbook of a different car altogether and said it was "probably more accurate".

Road Signs

One criticism aimed at our glorious nation is that we are forever living in the past. Well, it's hardly surprising when you take a look at some of our antique roadsigns. Many of them date back to the birth of motoring in the 1930s. Take a look at the warning sign for "Level Crossing Without Barrier Ahead". It's a steam locomotive in a red triangle! And what about "Level Crossing With Barrier Ahead", that's a pre-war level crossing gate in the form of a picket fence. Most of the people driving on the roads will never have seen either, yet still they live on. It's amazing that they've actually managed to get a jet into "Low Flying Aircraft" – you'd have thought a Tiger Moth would have been the obvious choice.

Most stupid of all is one that occurs the most frequently and that is the sign for a speed or traffic-lane camera. I can't be certain, but I have a suspicion that a wedding photographer's roll film camera has never been used to snap speeding cars at the roadside. Yet there it is, up on a roadside in all its anachronistic glory. The single-lens reflex camera gained popularity in the 1960s, this was superceded by the digital camera in the twenty-first century, but no, our representation of a camera is based on a 120 mm roll film device popular in the 1940s and 1950s. And while we're on the subject of roadsigns, why do we have to put up with having our hills measured in percentages? When I arrive at a hill and it says 15 per cent on the sign at the bottom I have no idea if I'm going to be grinding along in second gear at the top, or if the grumpmobile will take it at a canter. What we need is gradation on the lines of: Gentle, Quite Steep, Steep, Very Steep and Scary Steep.

Lycra Louts

These are the Lycra-clad cyclists with clip-in bike shoes, skinny tyres, who wear last year's Tour de France top. For some reason the little area in front of traffic lights specially reserved for cyclists is not enough for them and they'll go straight on through. Either that or they'll spend a minute blalancing on the pedals like some over-achieving circus dog. I don't want to start a national trend or anything, but when you're in front of them, your brakes are always going to be better than theirs...

GRUMP-
INSPIRED
DRIVING
PUNISHMENTS

Throughout this book, you have seen laid out for you what I would describe as the *First Grump Republic's Transport Manifesto* – what would be labelled in manifesto-speak as "the road ahead" (or as my wife might label it, "the long and winding grump"). The Grump Republic would administer Grumpia Law, many examples of which you have seen on earlier pages. We would institute the points-based car crusher scheme for inconsiderate parking and discourteous driving practices. A nice touch would be for the metal produced by the crusher to be reconstituted into a lovely pushbike as a lasting memento of the misdemeanor.

On top of all that, the Grump Department of Transport would be far more inventive about its punishments for bad drivers. If you're a bad driver and get fined or have points put on your licence for doing something stupid or antisocial then nobody will find out about it. Gone are the days when details of minor motoring offences were reported in the local paper. It's between you, the police computer and your licence. Though we have the glory of the crusher for cars driven without roadtax or insurance, there is no naming and shaming for drivers who have endangered others' lives by driving without due care and attention, or the necessary shame imposed on drunken drivers, unless, of course, there has been some horrendous headline-invoking consequence.

But if the Grumpy Avenger had his way, there would be. Some of the "Speed Kills" adverts on television have been very powerful of late, and the "Drink Driving" adverts in the run-up to Christmas get more gruesome by the year. I would like to add to this misery by printing a happy montage of the photos of persistent drunk drivers. I'm sure some Eurocrat will say it breaches their fundamental human rights, but I'd have a rogue's gallery of drunk drivers up there and wish them a happy Christmas.

On to the punishments...

Offence: Driving an illegally modified, custom car.
Punishment: Trial by safari park. The miscreant would have to park his vehicle for an hour in the monkey and

baboon enclosure and watch while all those eager prehensile fingers got to work at the expensive body fairings, the wheel trims, the wing mirrors, the aerials...

Offence: Speeding near a school.
Punishment: A fine, plus the car will be equipped with My Little Pony alloy wheels for a year (information to be logged onto the police computer). Every time the embarrassed motorist looks at his car, "Lickety Spit" will stare right back from every wheel arch. Hopefully in a judgemental kind of way.

Offence: Driving at speeds in excess of 100 mph.
Punishment: Car to be swapped for a G-Wiz electric car. It's the best-selling electric vehicle, which looks like it's either been badly squashed from front to back or escaped from a pre-school cartoon series. Their range is about 50 miles and their top speed makes a 2CV look like a Bugatti Veyron.

Offence: (Suggested by Mrs Grump) Parking in a dangerous position near a school, because the mother can't be arsed to get out and walk a little bit closer. Or her shoes don't do distance.
Punishment: Entire wardrobe is confiscated and the offender is given 30 yards of hessian, a Singer sewing machine and four zips. Now show up at the school gate and be fashionable.

Offence: Heavily polluting exhaust.
Punishment: A pipe from the exhaust will be fed back into the car with 30 per cent of the exhaust gases returning to the interior. See how you like it.

Offence: Frightening horses by driving too close/fast.
Punishment: Compulsory attendance to all seven days of the Horse of the Year show at Olympia. (Very unlikely to see repeat offenders after that.)

Offence: Driving over 50 mph in a 30 mph zone.
Punishment: The "Greensleeves" ice-cream van jingle will be fitted to the offender's car and will play continuously while the car is doing in excess of 30 mph. Which should make motorway trips interesting.

Offence: Driving without due care and attention.
Punishment: A serious offence deserves a serious punishment. The offender will have to pay for a towbar to be fitted to his car and will have to haul round an advertising trailer promoting a road safety message for a year. Thus, when he pulls up outside his house, his neighbours will know what a knob he's been. Alternatively, he can park it several streets away and put up with the inconvenience of walking to and from it every day. Genius.

Offence: Throwing cigarette butts, cans or litter onto the street.

Punishment: Stamp the words "LITTER BIN", plus the hand-throwing logo, onto the side of their car and use it as a litter bin for a day. Make sure children use it to dispose of plenty of chewing gum.

Offence: Parking in a disabled bay when the driver is clearly not disabled, or using an illegally obtained disabled sticker. (Anybody see that documentary with the husband of Cherie Blair's personal advisor? Him in particular.)
Punishment: The driver will be obliged to travel everywhere by wheelchair for a month and see if the lifestyle really suits them...

Offence: (Another from Mrs Grump) Parking in a "mother and toddler" bay at a supermarket when the owner clearly hasn't got a toddler with them. (Having one at home doesn't really count.)
Punishment: Technically, this isn't a motoring offence ("mother and toddler" spaces not being covered by the Highway Code). However, should they become part of the parking landscape then the punishment would be to look after one, having gone through a rigorous range of security checks first.

Offence: Using a hand-held mobile phone while driving.
Punishment: The phone would be taken off the driver and ceremonially thrown into deep water. There is nothing so satisfying as hearing the "plop" of an

expensive phone as it begins its long journey back to the sea. The owner is free to retrieve it if they wish.

Offence: Trailing football scarves out of the back windows of cars on the way to games.
Punishment: Drivers will be compelled to listen to Radio 5's post-match phone-in programme.

Offence: Keeping the Red Nose on your car two months (sometimes two years) after the Children in Need Red Nose Day appeal is finished.
Punishment: Levy a charge on the driver to be handed straight over to the next appeal. Whatever they paid for the Red Nose in the first place, that figure per month until the nose is removed. They're not going to object – after all, it's for charidee.

Offence: Failing to open your door and sideswipe a dog that chases your car on a country road. This is now obligatory for all visitors to the countryside. We have to teach them our city ways. Don't let John Craven convince you otherwise.
Punishment: Drivers will be compelled to watch all 36 series of *Dog Borstal*.